MW00886602

AN INSIGNIFICANT WOMAN

ONE WOMAN'S JOURNEY TO FIND A TRUTH

R. W. KAY

AN INSIGNIFICANT WOMAN
ONE WOMAN'S JOURNEY TO FIND A TRUTH

This is a work of fiction. All of the characters, names, incidents, organizations, and dialogue in this novel are either the products of the author's imagination or are used fictitiously.

iUniverse books may be ordered through booksellers or by contacting:

iUniverse
1663 Liberty Drive
Bloomington, IN 47403
www.iuniverse.com
844-349-9409

ISBN: 978-1-6632-1231-3 (sc)
ISBN: 978-1-6632-1229-0 (hc)
ISBN: 978-1-6632-1230-6 (e)

Library of Congress Control Number: 2021923684

Print information available on the last page.

iUniverse rev. date: 12/14/2021

1

It was 4:30 a.m. Sunday when Sarah Birch arrived home from her going-away party at DANNAR Biochemical Company. The evening festivities had begun early that spring night at Louie's Trattoria in Midtown Manhattan just east of Thirty-Ninth and Third Avenue, directly across from the DANNAR corporate offices, Sarah's work home for the last three years. Louie's Trattoria was the debriefing spot most days after work. Generally, debriefing sessions were fun, while also filled with occasional comments about how to revamp the company and change a variety of its rules and regulations. Tonight, however, the mood had been somber, as one of the well-loved members of the firm was leaving. No one understood the motivation behind Sarah's sudden decision to leave such a well-paying job, one she seemed to love. But that was Sarah!

When the evening began, everyone felt a bit distressed over the fact that such a well-liked and well-qualified person was leaving. But as the evening progressed, as with most going-away parties, the night wore into the morning, and the mood generated feelings more inspired by what the participants thought. The alcohol probably had something to do with that.

"Think you made a wise move," one of Sarah's coworkers, Jayne Goodwin, said as her long blonde-gray hair gently fell over one of her two fire-red eyes.

"You do, do you? And why do you think that?" Sarah was feeling the same amount of pain as Jayne was from the dirty gin martinis the bartender at Louie's had mixed, making sure all glasses were full throughout the evening.

"Well, it's obvidious," Jayne began.

"You mean *obvious*, Jayne; I think that's the word you're seeking."

"You're right. You're damn right. It is obvious," Jayne mumbled as she began to slink down into Louie's plush, maroon leather booths.

"OK, I'll bite. What's so obvious that I should leave DANNAR?" Sarah responded, using the company's literal pronunciation.

"Well, you know I've been there for almost forty years, and I remember how we started," she began.

Sarah, being very interested in Jayne's knowledge and her long seniority with the company, decided to sit down and listen to Jayne's story. "OK, Jayne, I'm all ears, but before you begin, I need a refill. How about you?" Sarah already knew the answer to that question, but the party protocol required it to be covered.

"Jamie, a couple more over here for me and my friend."

"Coming right up, Sarah," Jamie replied. "Same as before with the three olives?"

"Si, senor. Maybe a few more hors de oeuvres also. I think Jayne might like some."

Jamie set the drinks down on the table, and Jayne tipped him generously.

"Thank you, Jayne!" Jamie replied, showing the utmost gratitude. "But this is Sarah's night, and it's a pleasure to serve at her going-away party. She is going to make this big city a colder place."

"Why, thank you, Jamie," Sarah said. "That's very nice of you to say." Jamie turned and made his way back to the bar, but it was clear that he harbored great feelings for Sarah, as did most people at the party.

"All right, Jayne, what is there about the company I don't already know?" Sarah eyed her raconteur with her right eye, the one that still retained the look of a sober former employee.

"Sarah," Jayne quietly and pointedly said. "I admire you getting out of DANNAR while you can still have a career elsewhere." Jayne continued to commend Sarah for her resignation.

"You know, Sarah, I admire you,' Jayne repeated.

"I know, Jayne. You said that just a few moments ago," Sarah said, showing a bit of lethargy in her retort.

"I did. Oh, I'm so sorry. I think I had a little too much to drink." Jayne belched.

"No, no. You're fine, Jayne," Sarah replied with a quintessential professorial look at an ailing student. "What were you about to say?"

"Oh yes," Jayne continued. "You're a bright girl, Sarah, so don't be like me. You see, I, too, was bright when I first came to DANNAR. In those days, my educational accomplishments far exceeded most of the males indoctrinated into the company."

"And what happened?" Sarah asked after Jayne fell silent, tears welling in her eyes.

"Well, they all moved ahead, some up and out and some just up in the DANNAR hierarchy." Jayne sobbed. "And here am I, living proof of a lack of opportunity for women."

"But, Jayne," Sarah said, "this is the twenty-first century. There are numerous paths open to the women who want to fight sexual discrimination, if that's what you're referring to."

"You're right, Sarah, and more power to the woman who does fight those battles. For me, I'm an old-timer. I always thought fairness wills out."

Sarah sat there in amazement at Jayne's story and the naivete of the last statement. If it were not for Sarah's persona non grata, by tomorrow morning, Jayne's situation would be on her to-do list with upper management. She always felt that a labor leader might have been a calling she should have pursued.

"Just out of curiosity, Jayne, what's your educational background?" Sarah asked.

"I have two degrees, one in microbiology and a master's in organic chemistry."

"Impressive," Sarah said. "And where did you receive those degrees?"

Sarah kept the dialogue rolling for fear that silence would put Jayne back into her remorse, sobbing.

"My undergraduate degree is from Bryn Mawr, and my master's degree is from Harvard," Jayne responded.

"Harvard!" Sarah said. "I'm impressed."

"Yes, I thought the world would be my oyster, particularly after studying at those schools. But here I am, still a techie at DANNAR, making E. coli cells from lettuce leaves so we can torture germs, while compounding statistical data for some pimpled millennial creep who thinks the world owes him a living."

"Jesus," Sarah said quietly.

"That's why I made that statement earlier about getting out of this place. It'll eat you up," Jayne said. "You'll go along for a while, enjoying the ride, and then one day it's too late. As I said before, you're brilliant, Sarah. With your educational background, a Nobel Prize nomination for research at such a young age, and your looks, why, you're a shoo-in for success at a company that will appreciate your talents."

"How do you know about the prize nomination for research?" Sarah asked.

"Honey," Jayne said, with a grin that could reach from the Trattoria to the banks of the Hudson River, "when you're with a company as long as I've been with DANNAR, you know the ins and outs of its workings. You know where all the skeletons are buried and just about anything you can name. I peeked at your file."

That's interesting, Sarah thought. *Too bad the upper echelon of the company didn't also peek.*

"Listen," Jayne said, controlling her liquor as best as possible, "wherever you finally wind up, if you ever need any information about what DANNAR is doing, just call."

Sarah was taken aback. "Isn't that tantamount to industrial espionage, Jayne? You could get into a whole lot of trouble, including jail time, giving out information of the kind I suspect you're offering."

"As I said," Jayne responded, "*any*. I'm getting too old to care."

Just then, a cry rang out across the room.

"Whatever happened to the Shakespearean tragedy of how our lovely company came to be?" someone called out from the bar.

"Now, as for the company's start," Jayne said, elevated by the attention directed her way, "we did some unusual things sometime in the sixties, about the same time Masters and Johnson were gaining their notoriety."

The latter comment drew more attention from the increasing audience.

By the look on Sarah's face, she was having a difficult time recalling the names.

"You know, the book about human sexual response, or something like that," Jayne said, slurred.

"Oh yes, I do remember discussing them in medical school. Weren't they into identifying the impact sexual arousal has on human organs?" Sarah said, sounding like a student on her first day of class when asked if she had read the assignment.

"And" Jayne continued, "before they got into that study, they were into artificial insemination."

"Oh, I didn't know that." Sarah raised her glass as if toasting to that aspect of their business.

"Wait, you mean that DANNAR got its start providing artificial insemination, the same as Masters and Johnson?" someone called out, the crowd slowly growing in response to Jayne's narrative.

"Both," Jayne replied.

Sarah and others began questioning Jayne about her stories. Jayne's diatribe was quickly becoming the highlight of the evening.

"You mean we went from ways of inserting sperm to ways of breaking down DNA into individual parts, eliminating the necessity in the future of having two individuals involved in procreation?" one of the techs asked.

"Is that what you were working on when you decided to call it quits, Sarah?" someone asked.

"No, not something so sophisticated as that. Are we pursuing mono gene/chromosome splicing to do that? Is this possible? That's one reason I'm leaving. There are too many projects that are so secretive you practically need a CIA clearance to be accepted."

"It looks like it's going to be possible, Sarah. Why don't you withdraw your resignation and stay?" a voice called out.

A chant began. "Yes, Sarah, stay!"

At that moment, the senior vice president of research at DANNAR, who was sitting in a booth near the bar, chimed in, saying, "I think that's enough talking about DANNAR's sophisticated or not sophisticated private projects."

A hush fell over the crowd, a silence like a child retreating after being disciplined.

"OK, let's get back to DANNAR's start if we can't talk about what we're presently doing," someone said.

"So, who were they inseminating?"

"Well, generally, it was wives of husbands who had trouble," Jayne said.

"What kind of trouble? Couldn't get it up?" came a ridiculous question from someone hoping to catch Mr. Hill's attention.

"OK, gang, I know you've had a little hooch, but let's act a little less high schoolish."

"So come on, Jayne," one secretary began. "Finish your story about how DANNAR got its start."

"That's about it," she replied.

"No. How or where did the company obtain the super ethanol to make the situation a positive experience?" another tech said.

"He means sperm, Jayne," someone called out.

"Oh *that*," Jayne said, somewhat embarrassed. "Well, mainly from kids at the university,"

"There had to be some system to get a donor. What did they do—advertise in the newspaper?" the same tech asked as the audience, growing larger, began laughing.

"College kids always need money, and our secretary had a good relationship with several members of the football team and kids on fraternity row. She recruited them and offered them a stipend for every donor they could provide," Jayne said, enjoying being the center of attention.

"So how did it work? Did someone tell some jock that they needed someone to provide a specimen and leave it up to him as to who the donor would be?" asked someone in the back of the room.

"Yeah! How did the donor do it? Whack off on Sunday and walk into DANNAR on Monday with a condom full of the secret weapon?" came another supercilious question.

"No," she replied, taking a sip of her dirty martini. "They had a very sophisticated system of contacting individuals who would pick out students, develop a dossier, and set up a time the selected student would deliver his package."

"Did the woman or her husband ever know where the donation came?" asked a secretary, toning the group down.

"No, I don't think there were records kept in those days," Jayne responded, beginning to feel this was no longer storytelling but instead an inquisition.

"What about the dossiers kept by the student who solicited the donor?" Sarah asked.

"They were the property of the student who arranged the delivery. He only kept things like the color of eyes, race, religion, major, and things like that."

"How long did this go on? And how many women were impregnated?" someone asked.

"Several years, and I could only guess that somewhere in the neighborhood of three to four hundred plus woman had children as a result."

"Wow," Sarah said. "That means there are about four hundred adults out there, not too much older than I am, who will never know who their father is!"

"Hope they don't all try using Twenty-Three and Me," a tech quipped. "They're in for a real surprise."

Yes, they are, thought Sarah. *They're in for a real surprise!*

2

The previous night's festivities were still on Sarah's mind as she prepared to pack her belongings. New York had been everything she thought it would be, but it was now time to search for something new—her biological parents.

Anxious to begin this new chapter in her life, one comment that had been made the previous evening stuck with her and kept repeating its refrain: "They're going to be in for a big surprise."

They may not be able to find the identity of their father, she thought, *but at least they'll know who their mother is and her family line. I don't know the real identity of either of my parents.*

"This could be a long search," she mused.

Sarah had been raised as an orphan and never given any indication of who her parents were. What records she was able to find indicated she was placed on the doorsteps of Saint Anthony's Church in St. Louis, Missouri, almost twenty-nine years ago. From there, she was sent by the monks to St. Joseph's Orphanage, where she spent the first nine years of her life before Jim and Adrianne Birch adopted her.

At first, living with the Birches proved difficult. The newness and differences from Saint Joseph's regimen were not what the sisters had taught her. The sisters of St. Joseph had indoctrinated her: there was a right way and a wrong way for everything. Should one decide the wrong way, one would suffer either in this life or the next.

That training scared young Sarah so much, as it was a daily regimen when she began her elementary education at the new church, Saint Dominic's parish school.

The incongruences of her education, the nuns' teachings at the orphanage, and her new family life were so great that friction sometimes followed.

"Sarah, it's all right to be wrong occasionally," Jim Birch would often say. "Don't worry so much."

But precision had been embedded in Sarah, and that concept would remain her hallmark characteristic until her entrance into secondary education. The change from the parochial education system to the public school system had an even more significant impact. The reason for the change was her desire for perfection. Cleveland High School offered the opportunity to take courses in medical dosimetry, something she found exciting.

But convincing her parents to allow a change from the religious aspect of Saint Dominic's High School to Cleveland's liberalization was not going to be an easy task. However, Sarah prevailed, using her perfectionism to her advantage, and she changed from a conservative to a liberal education.

Aside from the medical dosimetry courses, Cleveland High School (CHS) was a complete 180-degree change from Saint Dominic's. Studying and being prepared for class was at the student's discretion. No one demanded that you know the subject matter. Nor did anyone cut your knuckles with a hickory stick or ruler if you failed to prepare. No, the system required the student to learn what they wanted and disregard the rest.

In addition to academics, the school had a social system complete with sororities and fraternities. These provided the student knowledge of the social graces required by their membership and society at large.

Sarah enjoyed her experiences at CHS. The sorority that chose her, Gamma Omega Chi, taught her respect for a well-rounded spirit to prepare her for university life.

Sarah graduated magna cum laude from Cleveland and went on to be accepted at Washington University in St. Louis, deferring scholarships to other well-known schools like Stanford, Arizona, Temple, Johns Hopkins, and the University of London.

The Birch family was elated with this decision, as it kept her close to home. Washington University (Wash U), often called the Harvard of the Midwest, offered Sarah a full scholarship. The ability to live on campus while being close to home was the best of both worlds for Sarah.

Remarkably similar to her secondary school life, Sarah breezed through her collegiate curriculum. One summer night at the Thurtene Carnival, a fraternity/sorority-sponsored event for raising cancer research funds, she met Jim Jacobs from the Kappa Alpha fraternity and fell madly in love. The affair lasted almost two years until the two parted ways. Jim went to Johns Hopkins to study the aging process under the talented Dr. David Schlesinger, while Sarah remained at Washington.

It was upon her graduation that companies began interviewing students on campus. One company, DANNAR, was interested in Sarah and made an offer to have her start as a staff assistant, an eighteen-month training program in their Illinois operation.

As exciting as the position sounded, Sarah had other ambitions. Offers had come from schools like Stanford, Harvard, and even Washington University Medical School for full-ride scholarships and grants to pursue her field of endeavor.

Jim and Adrianne were heartbroken when Sarah chose Stanford University. She was, after all, their only daughter, and the pain caused by her inevitable move was immense.

After graduate school and the completion of her dissertation for her PhD concomitant with her MD, DANNAR reapproached her, offering her the position of senior research analyst in Midtown Manhattan. She accepted the offer along with the lucrative salary. Her office, relatively small by her salary standards, was in the research division. Her initial assignment was to work on a highly specialized and confidential program of human regeneration. Her immediate and initial charge concerned breaking down the cell wall to determine how cancer could jump from one cell to another and leave the wall intact. She accomplished this with great enthusiasm and ultimately was nominated for the Nobel Prize in Research; however, she was not selected. Still, the honor of being nominated was the highlight of her career with DANNAR. Less than a year after the nomination, she decided it was time to leave DANNAR for a new adventure.

Years ago, Sarah had received some curious results through Twenty-Three and Me regarding potential relatives, and it was something she had always wanted to dive deeper into. Having completed due diligence phone calls and interviews, she had narrowed her search down to two likely relative candidates. One lived in Kansas City, and the other in a small town in Nebraska.

Thanks to DANNAR's generous salary, she found herself in a position to be able to devote at least one year to chasing her lifelong dream of finding her parents.

3

Concentrating on her two last alternatives from the Twenty-Three and Me potential cousins report, Sarah made several phone calls to a Jonathon Banks in Stillwater, Nebraska. It appeared as though there had been no definitive connection between the two, as Mr. Banks could recite his family history back to the range wars, and no room existed for a long-lost second cousin on his mother's side of the family. His father had no siblings, eliminating that potential. That left only one remaining possibility, George Hartman of Overland Park, Kansas, a well-to-do suburb of Kansas City, Missouri.

Sarah obtained as much information about George as she could from details on Google, Facebook, and other social media outlets. She knew he, too, had been orphaned at an early age and had searched for his biological parents for a time. Sarah hoped that his quest was far more complete than her own. If only he had been fortunate enough to find his mother, she reasoned, and he was, in fact, her second cousin, his mother could be her mother's sister. The thought of that possibility was exciting to Sarah.

The flight to Kansas City took a little over three and a half hours due to severe weather along the route, somewhere over Illinois's skies. The weather caused the pilot to announce that a time delay was inevitable due to the alternate routing south around Saint Louis and the destination area.

His bedside manner from the cockpit was exceptional, making the delay more palatable, especially when he included that he was offering free drinks for the passengers.

"And what would you like?" asked the flight attendant.

"What? I'm sorry, what did you ask?" Sarah replied, having been engrossed in her biological and factual study of the person who would be her second cousin.

"Would you like a drink on the captain?" the flight attendant said while observing the papers and the family tree and charts Sarah had spread out over two seats.

"Oh, yes, excuse me," Sarah said. "I was deeply involved in my reading!"

"So I observed," the attendant replied. "What would you like?"

"Do you have any champagne?" Sarah asked, not expecting a positive response. "I'm celebrating, and a glass of the bubbly is just the thing to set it off."

"Well, in that case, champagne it is," the efficient, personable hostess replied before she retreated to the galley.

After delivering the drink, the flight attendant was very interested in Sarah's research. While Sarah sipped champagne, she explained the papers and her situation.

"I'm extremely interested in what you're doing, as I'm an adopted child myself and still would like to know something about who I am, where I came from, and, my history," the flight attendant confessed.

Sarah slipped into her dissertation mode, explaining how she had come to this moment.

The flight attendant told Sarah she wanted to learn more and asked Sarah if she would consider having a drink with her while in Kansas City. Vickie, as her TWA name tag indicated, and Sarah exchanged contact information.

"I'll be staying at the Crown Center Plaza," Sarah announced while gathering up her papers and placing them neatly in her Gucci leather attaché case.

The captain made a smooth landing at the KCI Airport. The ride from the airport to Crown Center seemed longer than the flight, thanks to Vickie's attentiveness. Sarah was happy to have made a friend in the Kansas City area. *Who knows? Maybe she could be of some help.*

Two days passed before a telephone call from Vicki came through the Crown Center's front desk.

"Hello, Vicki," Sarah said with excitement in her voice, indicating she was glad to receive her call.

"How is the search going?" Vicki asked. "Did you find your cousin?"

"Well, my cousin, if he's truly my cousin, seems to be a little bit of a bon vivant. He's tough to nail down."

"That's too bad," Vicki replied. "Would you like to meet for a drink or dinner tonight? I know the KC area pretty well, and maybe I can help you corral this cousin of yours."

"Sounds good," Sarah said, hoping the added assistance would help determine his whereabouts.

"OK, how about if I pick you up at six thirty and we make our way over to the Herford House for drinks and dinner? And then it's down to Country Club Plaza for some fine Kansas City–style nightlife. It will do you well!" Vickie said.

The remainder of the evening was about Sarah's search rather than meeting the male sector of Kansas City, a potential goal Vickie had set.

"Tell me, Sarah. We've been talking most of the evening about this guy that's your supposed cousin, but you have yet to reveal his name," Vickie said, looking over her chocolate martini at Eddie's Chateau La Bouffe, a downtown nightspot.

"Oh." Sarah hiccupped. "Yes, his name is Hartman—George Hartman."

"I used to know a guy named George Hartman. He was a senior when I was a junior in high school," Vickie said with a look of *I told you I knew a lot of people in the area.*

"Do you think you know this guy?" Sarah said.

"I might. Where did he go to school?"

"According to Facebook, he was on the Raiders' football team. Just a minute, and I'll have the name of the high school." Sarah searched through her notes.

"Don't bother." Vickie smiled. "It's Shawnee Mission High School South."

"You do know him!" Sarah said.

"Hold it just a minute, Sarah. Slow down. I didn't say I know him. It's more like I know *of* him. He was a big football jock when I was in school. I think he was the big man on campus, the heartthrob of all the girls, especially the cheerleaders."

"Can you get in touch with him? Where does he live? Do you know where he hangs out?" Sarah fired question after question at Vickie.

"I might know a couple of old school mates that could get in touch with him and possibly set up a meeting," Vickie said. "But what do I say to get him interested in talking to you?"

Tell him anything, Sarah thought, then hit upon an idea. "Tell him this good-looking girl saw him the other evening and wants desperately to make his acquaintance."

"That's not a very novel idea," Vickie replied. "It's as old as the Garden of Eden."

"Can' you think of anything better than that?" Sarah chided the knowledgeable flight attendant.

"I'll try." Vickie winked at Sarah, seeing the excitement in her eyes rise to the level of vitality.

Vickie dropped Sarah back at the Crown Center, indicating she would get on the phone as soon as she returned home.

Two and a half hours later, Sarah's hotel telephone rang. It was Vickie.

"We're in luck," Vickie said. "He's willing to meet you."

"Fantastic! What did you say to him?"

"Nothing. I didn't talk with him. A good friend of mine who's a good friend of his did the talking."

"And what did he say?" Sarah wanted to know.

"I don't know, and what difference does it make? You've got your meeting," Vickie replied.

"You're right." Sarah thanked Vickie and then wanted to know the particulars.

"I have an overnight tomorrow with a layover in Miami, so I made the arrangements for the following evening. I thought you might want me with you, and I want to be there!" Vickie was now anxious to see this old heartthrob. "So, I'll pick you up about the same time as I did tonight. It's only about a ten-minute drive to the River Quay and Papa Nick's Bar and Restaurant, one of your cousin's hangouts.

"Super!" Sarah said. "And thanks for all your help, Vickie. I sincerely mean it."

"Nothing at all. Piece of cake," Vickie said, smiling. "Dinner and drinks are on you. I think that's the least you can do."

"Agreed! See you in two nights."

4

As sure as counting on TWA's on-time performance, Vickie arrived at the hotel drive at the time scheduled, awaiting Sarah's appearance.

"Well, hello, stranger," she greeted Sarah, who looked as if she was going on her first high school date. "Relax. This is going to be your big night. Just think. The search may come to an end tonight."

"Oh, I hope you're right," Sarah replied, peeking in the rearview mirror, making sure her makeup was perfect.

"OK. Here's the plan for this evening," Vickie said. "We should get there about half an hour before your cousin, if my sources are correct. I understand he usually hangs out at Papa Nick's every Wednesday and Thursday from about six thirty to ten o'clock. That should give us ample time to get there before him, get prepared, and then make our move—or should I say *your* move."

"Great," Sarah responded. "But how will we know him?"

"Oh, don't worry, Sarah. If I remember him from school days, he'll be easy to spot," Vickie said with a wink. "Don't forget. I said he was gorgeous."

Ten minutes later, the two ladies exited the car and made their way into the secluded nightclub, restaurant, and bar. Upon entering the establishment, Sal Arellano, the owner, greeted everyone. He was a mild-mannered man whose recent move from New York to Kansas City indicated rumblings within the family. The newspapers said Sal had a particular penchant for fixing problems.

"Good evening, ladies," Sal said. "May I offer you a table, or would you prefer a seat in the lounge?"

Quick on her feet, Vickie responded, "How about both?"

"Both?" Sal seemed perplexed.

"You know, a nice dinner table with a marvelous view of the lounge." Vickie winked. "Just in case something interesting appears."

Sal grinned. "I have just the place for you." He winked as he put them at table number five overlooking the bar below.

"Hope your evening is enjoyable," Sal said before the head waiter, accompanied by a busboy, came to greet them and take their drink orders.

"Johnnie Walker Black with a splash of water for me," Vickie ordered.

"And for you, ma'am?"

"Do you have champagne?" Sarah asked.

"Of course. We have Dom Perignon Vintage, Bollinger James Bond 007, Moet & Chandon, Taittinger, and Freixenet Condon Negro Brut," the waiter rattled off. "Which would you like?"

Sarah glanced over to Vickie with a look of *What language is he speaking?*

"She will be glad to have the Freixenet," Vickie said to the waiter.

"And will that be a bottle or flute?" came the follow-up question.

"I think she better start with a flute, and we can increase later."

"Very good, madam," the waiter said as he departed the table.

"What did you order, Vickie?" Sarah asked, her alleged New York sophistication lacking.

"Well, I ordered you a nice quasi-champagne reasonably priced. He started at about two hundred eighty dollars per bottle and slowly came down from there. At that price, one glass would have cost about fifty dollars a flute. I just adjusted the bill of fare to about twelve dollars for an as-if champagne, and believe me, you won't know the difference."

About halfway through their dinner, a handsome young man walked past their table, and Sarah, upon seeing him, said to Vickie, "Jesus, that guy is good-looking!"

"He is, isn't he, and you know something? He looks a little bit like you. Yes, there is a vague resemblance. I bet he could be your maternal second cousin!" Vickie raised her eyebrows in a motion of *There he is.*

"That's him?" Sarah asked in disbelief. "What do I say? How should I approach him?" Sarah, showing signs of nervousness, swallowed deeply.

"Don't worry. I've got it all figured out," Vickie said. "I'll go into the lounge and reintroduce myself as an acquaintance from high school. That should give me time to BS for a while about old acquaintances, the Green and Gold, the school, and then work my way into the fact that I have a friend at the table who is dying to meet him. After I introduce the two of you, the rest is your bag."

Vickie left the table and made her way into the lounge. After about forty-five minutes, she and George Hartman entered the dining room and made their way to the table where Sarah waited. The rendezvous was not quite what George had expected. Rather than finding a quasi-schoolgirl who had designs on him, he found someone in her late twenties, sophisticated, impeccably dressed, and showing signs of familiarity only a relative might comprehend.

Vickie's introduction left no room for George to fail to understand the reason for the meeting. It was well established that Sarah was searching for a cousin, and from her past research, she believed George to be in the ninety-eight-percentile range of being that relative.

"What's the reason for the search?" George asked.

Sarah shared a biography of her life and a dissertation on her rationale for finding her biological parents.

"I noticed on Facebook that you had been searching for your parents. Did you ever find them?"

"No, not them," George responded in a staccato voice. "I found her," he said.

The excitement grew as Sarah realized her mother's identity might be only a few more sentences away.

The thrill and effervescence of being so close yet so far away from reaching a close to her search made Sarah want to fire off a thousand questions. However, she did not want George to think she only cared for herself. Instead, she covered areas of concern to both her and George, culminating in, "What's your mother's name?"

"Oh yes, that," George replied. "Her name is Sister Mary Theresa, and since you're so interested, at the Grotto of Mary Magdalene."

"Do you know, does your mother have a sister?" Sarah's voice was quivering as she spoke.

"Yes, she does," George responded, showing signs of being on turf he did not want to tread.

"Where does she live? Close by? Do you see her often? Does her sister live close? What is her sister's name?" came the rapid-fire interrogation, as she slowed down only to take a sip of her flute of Freixenet.

"My mother lives in France—Provence, France," he said. "At the shrine of Mary Magdalene."

"Does your mother's sister live in France also?"

"I'm not sure, Sarah. I do know they both were in Rome together at one time," he said. "But beyond that, I don't know anything."

"Well, George, how did you feel meeting your mother after all the searching you did?" Sarah probed.

Rather than respond, George excused himself and made his way to the restroom, an effort to regroup and consider what he would say during the remainder of Sarah's interrogation. When he returned, he sat down and immediately began talking, as if he had found his voice.

"Sorry, Sarah," he began. "But there's something fucked up about this entire situation. Something tells me you might be better off stopping your search here and now."

"Why?" came an incredulous reply. "I've come this far. What could be so frightening?"

George looked around the dining room to see if anyone was listening. His demeanor changed from the outgoing bon vivant to someone who appeared troubled with guilt.

"So come on, George. What's the story?" Sarah asked as she clasped his hands in hers, a doctor's way of instilling confidence in the other person.

"Well," George began, "I'm Catholic, as I suppose you are. I've been Catholic all my life. So what I'm about to tell you shakes the foundations of my belief to the core."

"This is all from your research?" Sarah asked.

"Yes, from my research—but more from my actual meeting with my mother," George responded.

"So, you found her and met with her. How wonderful for you!"

"Not necessarily," George said.

"What did you say? What did she say? You were probably speechless." Sarah gushed with excitement.

"Yes, Sarah, I met her," George said.

Sarah waited in anticipation of George's identification of a joyous encounter, but it never came.

"She never married." George sadly peered into his glass of beer. "I guess that makes me some sort of ..."

"Oh." Sarah looked away. "I'm sorry. Did she give you any information regarding the identity of your father, or does that require further research?"

"No, Sarah, I won't be pursuing it any further," George replied with a case-closed look on his face.

"Why not? You're so close."

"Because ..." he started. "Because, Sarah, my mother was a nun when I was born. She is still of the cloth, following some zealot cult of Mary Magdalene."

"Oh my God," Sarah said. "Was your father a priest?" Tears began rolling down her face, either in empathy for his feelings or what might be her fate.

"No, I wish that were the case. My mother was, according to her story, artificially inseminated ritually by church people."

"What?" Sarah shrieked, loud enough to draw others' attention not only in the dining room but also the lounge area.

After the crowd's consternation subsided, it became apparent that she and George could use another drink.

"Another drink, George?" she questioned. "Maybe something with a little more bite than the Bud Light you've been nursing?"

"Yes, please," George replied. "I'll take a Stolie straight up. It's good for stories like this, wouldn't you say?" He looked at Sarah with pleading eyes that harbored a deep-seated dislike of the story he had uncovered.

"I imagine so," Sarah reluctantly replied as she flagged down the waiter. She ordered two Stolies straight up.

"Give this to me again," she requested. "Your mother was a nun of the Catholic Church, and she was impregnated how?"

"Artificially, as I understand it," George said just before shooting the Stolie delivered by the waiter.

"Why?"

"I don't know. Needless to say, I'm not in a position to know the answer to that question." George signaled the waiter for a refill of his Russian vodka drink. Turning to Sarah, he continued, "Thanks to the vigorous search of my wonderful family tree, something I should have left alone, I am now in a position of having lost my faith. This is all because of finding my mother, the church, and the fact they would throw the product of whatever they were doing, me, into an orphanage like a piece of unwanted trash. Fuck them! Fuck them."

George became extremely reluctant to continue and retreated as if he had just blasphemed against the only staple of his life, the church.

"I'm sorry if my questions upset you, George, but I'm on the same quest you found yourself on when you went to Provence. Now it seems to be my turn to travel abroad and see if I can unravel the puzzle you laid before me."

After this, the parties bid one another farewell, exchanged telephone numbers and addresses, and vowed to continue this dialogue later.

On the way back to the hotel, Sarah turned and asked Vickie, "Do you believe the story George put on the table?"

Shaking her head, Vickie responded, "It's incredulous; it's not normal, that's for sure. When I think back on my Catholic upbringing, I thought the nuns were chaste and incapable of sin or incapable of being involved in something as sordid as this. But, Sarah, if your mother is this woman's sister, was she also a nun? If so, I would wonder if my mother was also impregnated. And why? For what reason?"

"I don't know, but unlike George, I have to find the answer, not only for my lineage edification but for the riddle placed at my feet. It seems, Vickie, the only way I can find some of these answers is to go to Provence, France, and see where the trail leads. Does TWA fly to Provence, France?" Sarah inquired of Vickie.

"Hell, I don't even know where Provence, France, is, much less whether we fly there or not," Vickie said. "But by this time tomorrow, I will know, and if my contacts are as good as they used to be, I will secure first-class accommodations for you."

"Can you do that?" Sarah inquired.

"Of course. You paid for my dinner and gave me drinks and a questionable story to boot. That's the least I can do for my new friend," came Vickie's wide-eyed reply.

"Fantastic," Sarah said. "I've never flown first class before. That should be a new experience."

"Speaking of new experiences, you alluded to George's mother, the nun, being a follower of Mary Magdalen. What's that all about? I mean, a Catholic nun following a wayward woman?"

"I know," Sarah responded. "When I was in grade school, Mary Magdalen was portrayed by the sisters of St. Mary's as a prostitute who had broken each of the seven deadly virtues. I don't know where this is going, but it appears as though my research will become a little more interesting once I reach Provence. Only time will tell."

5

True to her word, Vickie arranged for Sarah's upgrade to first class on her flight from Kansas City International to New York's John F. Kennedy Airport. The layover in New York was almost six hours, from four o'clock until ten o'clock that evening, before flight 800 departed for Paris, France.

Somehow, Vickie had planned with the JFK gate agent to upgrade Sarah to TWA's First-Class Royal Ambassador Service.

The flight took a little over six hours and fifty minutes, arriving at Paris Charles de Gaulle Airport at 7:50 a.m., Paris time. Along the way, Sarah enjoyed a sumptuous meal of chateaubriand complemented by her favorite bottle of Freixenet, which had been sent by her new and devoted friend Vickie.

"Best of luck, and may your research bring happiness," the card attached to the bottle of quasi-champagne read. Vickie had made a tremendous impression upon Sarah, and Sarah wrote in her diary to find an authentic Parisian Louis clutch as a thank you for all she had done.

Because of the inbound flight from Lyons being late, the Air France flight from Charles de Gaulle to Marseilles, scheduled to depart at 9:45 a.m., was delayed. This added time gave Sarah a little more opportunity to study the notes she had made during her conversation with George. She enjoyed superb beignets served at one of the main concourse cafés.

Precisely forty-five minutes later, three chimes and a sensuous female voice announced that the flight to Marseilles was now boarding. Sarah scarfed down the last sip of coffee and made her way to the gate area. One hour and thirty-five minutes later, the aircraft was taxiing to the terminal.

The town of St. Maximin-la-Sainte-Baume, the location where George made the acquaintance of his nun mother, was about one hour from Marseille Airport. According to brochures Sarah had picked up at the airport, it was the town where Saint Mary Magdalene's grave was located. The Basilica of Saint Mary Magdalene was built over the crypt where her remains had been uncovered in 1295.

The Hostelries-de-la-Sainte-Baume, where Sarah had reservations, which were made by Vickie, was run by Dominican nuns, the same order as that of Sister Mary Theresa.

"Good afternoon," the nun greeted Sarah as she entered the hostelry. "You must be Ms. Sarah Birch from the good ole USA." The nun smiled warmly.

"Why yes, yes I am," Sarah replied. "How did you know that?"

"No, I'm not psychic." Sister Agnes smiled. "You see, it's a Thursday afternoon, and you're the only person scheduled to check in today, so I just guessed."

"Ah, yes, that's me," Sarah replied, feeling the warmth of Sister Agnes permeate the small entry foyer.

"Your American contact, a Miss Victoria, said you wished to rent a villa for two weeks. Is that correct?"

"Yes," Sarah said. "It seems as though there is a great deal to see in Provence, and I'd like to take it all in." Sarah smiled.

"I understand," Sister Agnes responded. "I have been here for almost fifteen years, and I still haven't seen everything."

After completing her registration, Sister Agnes showed Sarah to the villa.

"Are you sure it is the villa you want to rent?" Sister Agnes queried. "It seems so large for just one person. I hope I didn't get the reservation wrong."

"No, Sister, if my good friend Victoria made the reservation, I'm sure it will be all right," Sarah replied with a look of confidence.

"OK." The nun shook her head. "It's just that the villa has four bedrooms, one with a queen bed, two with a full bed in each, and one with twin beds. That's five beds." She laughed. "It also has four and a half bathrooms. Two of the bedrooms have en suite showers, and two separate toilets. There is a pool and a beautiful garden. The villa also includes internet, washing machine, dryer, flat-screen TV, CD and DVD-players, and a Hi-Fi system. So, tell me, are you expecting a large group of guests, or are you just one of those rich Americans who have nothing else to do with their money?" She laughed.

"Oh my gosh," Sara responded. "I think my friend made a mistake. Can we correct it?"

"Sure, not a problem. I will take care of it as soon as I return to the office, and we will have you moved to more suitable arrangements tomorrow." The nun and Sarah both had a big laugh over Vickie's faux pas.

The two continued conversing much of the afternoon, and when Sarah felt she knew Sister Agnes, she said, "Sister, since you've been here for fifteen years, would you happen to know Sister Mary Theresa?"

"Why, of course. Do you know Sister Theresa?" Agnes asked.

"No, not really. A friend of mine knows her. I was to say hello if I happened upon her," Sarah said, attempting to keep the ruse as close to the vest as possible.

"Normally, she's here during the week, but this week, she's at the cave," Agnes said.

"The cave?" Sarah asked.

"Yes, she's directly above us. The hostelry is located just below the Cave of Saint Mary Magdalene."

"Oh, yes, the cave. Just above us?"

"Yes, just above. If you go outside and look directly overhead, you can see the cave. The only problem is that it takes over half an hour to get up there. So, if you want to see Sister Mary Theresa, you'll have to hike your way up. I sure hope your legs are in shape. It's a steep climb."

The two chatted for the next hour, mainly about America, as Sister Agnes was interested in someday traveling to Chicago, the "gangster town" as she called it.

"I'm afraid I can't tell you a great deal about Chicago, as my hometown is St. Louis." Sarah smiled.

"Oh. St. Louis, the home of the birds. They're good!" Sister Agnes commented.

"You're a baseball fan?" Sarah smiled, thinking how much Americans take for granted.

"Yes, I have an autographed baseball from Stash Musial when he visited the pope. I've followed him ever since. That's about the same time they wanted me—" She abruptly stopped.

"You picked a good one to like. Stan Musial is my favorite also. He's one of the last ballplayers who played the game for fun. Today, the players are money hungry and less concerned with the fans. At one time, the hierarchy and the priests of the game were concerned with the fans, particularly the children. Today they want to make those children pay for an autograph. Nonsense," Sarah said.

"I know what you mean about the upper echelon expecting special favors and perquisites. It even happens in my profession. Being a nun is sort of like being a fan of the game. You're a witness but never can become more than you are—a nun, a woman," Agnes unexpectantly blurted out.

"You sound as though you're dissatisfied with being a nun, Sister Agnes," Sarah said.

"No, I guess I'm just a little tired and have a desire to travel to other countries. I apologize, Ms. Sarah. I didn't mean that the way it sounded," the sister replied.

"Tell me, Sister. Although I was raised Catholic, we never talked much about Mary Magdalene, as she was, at least in America, persona non grata. We didn't talk much about her because the church labeled her as a prostitute. How is it you worship her here in Provence?"

"That's a good question, and I'm sure you'll understand the answer during your visit here, but if you don't, I'll gladly explain it."

"That's fair, but how about one question?"

"OK. One question." Sister Agnes smiled, feeling a sister relationship developing between the two.

"What is the cult of Mary Magdalene?" Sarah pointedly asked.

"Well, that's not as demonic as it sounds. It's not a group of covert people running around secretly teaching the Gospel of Mary Magdalene."

"Well, why are the Dominicans, your order, so involved with Mary Magdalene as a penitent prostitute?"

"That could be a long story," Sister Agnes responded, "but I'll give it to you as I learned in the Dominican order. Our order was founded in 1216 and had, by 1295, unofficially adopted Mary Magdalen as its patron. This adoption coincided with the granting to the Dominicans of the supervision of the Magdalen pilgrimage sites of La Sainte-Baume and Saint-Maximin in Provence.

"The preaching of penance by the Dominicans was an immediate success. The sermons gave Mary Magdalen a new significance and heightened interest in her as both a penitent and a prostitute."

"So, it's not some underground group of people with unusual beliefs?" Sarah asked.

"Oh no," the nun replied, laughing. "We are believers that Christ endowed Mary Magdalene with the power to lead His new religion and that because of a male-dominated society, the apostles, led by Peter, and the church at the Council of Nicaea excluded her, her teachings, and her vision from the new Catholic religion. Additionally, in his 591 CE Easter sermon, Pope Gregory branded her as a prostitute, giving her the status the church and the general population believe.

"This concerted effort on the part of many expressly excluded women from positions of authority in the church, and as a result, it denied Mary Magdalene's vision of Christ's teachings. We believe that the first pope of the church should have been Mary Magdalene, not Peter."

"So, what's different about her teachings and those we perceive were related to Jesus? Why did some early Christians consider Mary Magdalene to be an apostle while others did not?" Sarah asked.

Sister Agnes shared her knowledge of the times of Mary. "Some Christian texts, both Orthodox and Gnostic, identify her role as one of the very first witnesses to the resurrection. They portray Mary Magdalene as the 'apostle to the apostles.' Other sources, particularly the Gospels of the New Testament, exclude or replace her in their resurrection accounts. The withholding of apostolic status operated as a tool of persuasion in the politics of early Christian literature. Canonical and noncanonical literature reveals intriguing correlations between Peter's prominence and a corresponding diminishment of Mary Magdalene—thus also a women's diminishing leadership and appointed place in the church."

"But that was a long time ago," Sarah pointed out. "What difference does it make today? Aren't the rules of engagement, so to speak, already drawn?"

"Catholics deserve to hear about the diversity of women in scripture. And reducing one of the most influential leaders of the early church to a prostitute has exacted a price, especially for women, by feeding into the notion that women are either a Madonna or prostitute.

"This study of early Christian tensions has severe implications for current denominational discourse because authority, apostolic status, and women's ordination continue to be highly disputed topics within Catholicism today. If we continue to visit false narratives upon our flock, how much longer will it be that our church as we know it self-implodes? Inquiring minds want to know!" Sister Agnes winked.

"Know what exactly?" Sara asked, knowing the question sounded simplistic.

Sister Agnes took the bait. Her enthusiasm caused her to restate in more detail her previous synopsis. "Women were leaders in the early Jesus movement. That fact is becoming accepted among scholars. Not only do several biblical passages describe them, but noncanonical writings also portray women as apostles and even deacons. Studies of ancient burial inscriptions also have confirmed these titles for women in the first century. Women played a prominent role in the Gnostic gospels, writings that provide crucial historical evidence about the first centuries' church.

"Did you know," she gushed like a schoolgirl, "the Gospel of Mary is the only text named for a woman? Mary Magdalene is a visionary who received concealed revelations directly from our Savior, much to the chagrin of Peter. Accordingly, in John 20, she was identified as someone who was a special channel of secret knowledge.

"According to Gnostic writings, shared leadership was practiced among Gnostic sects, with Mary of Magdala and other women figuring prominently. But as the early Christian church struggled for legitimacy, a male-dominated, hierarchical style of leadership prevailed. The gnostic materials are full of indications of opposition to Mary Magdalene's leadership," said Sister Agnes. "To put it simply, the people who opposed her won.

"Peter is the symbol of the church today, the power structure. At the same time, Mary Magdalene represents the pattern for the role of women. Much like your American system of democracy, two competing visions of the church were jockeying for position, and it's obvious which one won. Women were already subordinated. We, the Dominican members of the cult of Mary Magdalene, desire to change that mischaracterization."

"I thought you said earlier there was no such thing as the cult of Mary Magdalene," Sarah said.

"No, I said the cult of Mary Magdalene existed; what I failed to mention was that it existed about AD 1100," she quickly recanted. "I'm sorry, but I must get back to my chores before evening prayers. If you would like, we might continue our conversation sometime this week." She belied her offer by her fidgeting attempt at dusting a coffee table.

"Of course, Sister. I will look forward to that," Sara responded, believing that the faux pas made by Sister Agnes might preclude another meeting.

Something is odd, she thought. *Something is odd.*

6

The next morning, Sarah ventured to the foyer where she had met Sister Agnes the previous day. When she inquired of the nun's whereabouts, she was told that the sister had been sent to Paris to substitute in a teaching assignment for someone who had taken ill.

After a cup of French vanilla coffee and a powdered sugar beignet, Sarah asked for directions to the cave of St. Mary Magdalene.

A petite nun sitting behind the desk gave Sarah directions and admonished her to take her time and wear comfortable shoes, as the terrain was rugged.

Neither the nun at the foyer desk nor Sister Agnes had exaggerated the climb to the cave. It was both taxing and time-consuming. The final approach to the cave was a large staircase that Sister Mary Agnes had said would be taxing; however, once climbed, the area's aura would prove to have been worth the climb. The cave itself had a large opening covered by stained glass windows and a large door that was impressive in its appearance. Once inside, Sarah observed a variety of statues and altars dedicated to Mary Magdalene. Nonetheless, she thought it was still a cave—cool, damp, smelling of incense, earth, and rock dust.

Several nuns were milling around after the morning Mass had finished, and those on pilgrimage were beginning to make their way down the stairs just climbed by Sarah.

"Good morning, Sisters," she said as they finished genuflecting before the main altar.

Almost in unison, they responded, "Good morning."

Some made small talk as they departed the chapel. Sarah responded in kind.

"Excuse me, but could you indicate which of you is Sister Mary Theresa?" she questioned.

One of the nuns, apparently a novice dressed in a white habit, approached her. "The person you are looking for is the rectrix of our grotto, and she is presently in the office. It is located to the left of the altar and down the corridor on the left. You can't miss it," she cheerfully whispered.

"Thank you," Sarah bowed her head as if in adoration of the sisters, an old habit from her grade school days.

"You are very welcome," the young nun replied. "If I may be of any further assistance, please feel free to call on me. My name is Joan, the future Sister Joan." She smiled.

Once there, Sarah immediately sought out the nun called Sister Mary Theresa.

"Good morning, Sister. I understand you are the rectrix of this magnificent shrine to Mary Magdalene," Sarah began. "My name is Sarah Birch, and I'm the cousin of your son George Hartman. Your *son*," she reiterated, making quite sure her statement fell on the proper ears.

The ashen color of Sister Mary Theresa's face made it clear to Sarah that she had struck a nerve with her opening remark.

"Oh, yes, George Hartman," the nun replied. "How is George doing these days?"

Sarah then proceeded to tell her story, the reason she was in Provence and what she hoped to accomplish.

"I wish you luck in your endeavors," Theresa said with a sincerity that was pleasing to Sarah. "Sister Agnes informed me you would be coming to the cave to see me."

"She did?" Sarah looked somewhat surprised. "We had a long conversation yesterday when I checked in. Nice girl."

"Yes, she is," Sister Theresa said. "Sometimes, she is a little bit too talkative. Maybe that is why she's such a good teacher. Getting called off to Paris yesterday afternoon to fill in for a nun taken ill at the Dominican University was sudden, and she asked me to express her sorrow for missing you today."

"Being a good teacher, she gave me an excellent understanding of the modern-day cult of Mary Magdalene."

"She did say you were interested in that. May I ask why?"

"On the plane over, I did some last-minute catching up on my reading. I came across the cult of Mary Magdalene, and I had heard the expression recently in Kansas City, so I thought I would get an answer from someone daily involved with Saint Mary," Sarah, quick on her feet, replied.

"You may recall from your reading Pope Gregory's composite of Mary Magdalene and Mary of Egypt, identifying Magdalene as a prostitute. This negativity quickly assimilated into sermons and writings in the early Middle Ages. Soon after that, perhaps as early as the seventh century, there began to emerge the legend of Mary Magdalen that eventually produced a cult of great popularity. But that eventually dissipated," Sister Theresa said.

"So, is there a modern-day cult of Mary Magdalene?"

"No, not like the one you read identified. That one ended over a thousand years ago. Several years ago, however, a group of nuns formed a society using the name of the cult of Mary Magdalene, which was to identify with the saint and exemplify her love of the Savior, Jesus Christ. Again, there were no clandestine motives in using the word *cult*. Moreover, it was in tribute to those who had worshiped her many, many years ago. The group flourished among the Dominican nunnery, and due to their good deeds and charitable works, it drew the attention of some in Rome. As a result, the organization was contacted and asked to provide a special service to the church," Sister Theresa said.

"And would that be being impregnated through artificial means?" Sarah said.

"And where did you hear something like that, if I may ask?" the nun said, flashing signs of embarrassment.

"George Hartman," Sarah responded without hesitation.

"George Hartman. Oh yes, George!" Sister Mary Theresa repeated with a glint of pride in her eyes.

"So," Sarah said, "is that where the discussion of artificial insemination enters the Magdalene cult?"

"Well, somewhat," Sister Theresa responded, looking a little bit guilty. "I see you have been talking at some length with George. I told him this same story several years ago when he came to visit," she acknowledged.

"Yes, I have, and I must admit he is in a quandary over the entire situation. But he could not fill in many of the blank parts of the story, so I hope you will continue," Sarah said, using her best negotiation efforts to keep the nun talking. "What was the purpose of the artificial insemination?"

"I'm not sure if artificial insemination is the correct terminology," Sister Mary Theresa began. "It was more like surrogating. We acted as surrogate mothers for those who could not conceive or carry a child to maturity."

"So, is that the reason you and my mother gave the children away immediately after delivery?" Sarah probed, knowing the question would elicit a truth or a lie. In either event, she had prepared the next question.

"Well, yes and no," Sister Theresa said, recognizing this guest was forcing her to give more information than she had intended. "We thought we were doing a service for the mother church and that the child would be given to a needy Catholic family upon delivery."

"Did you ever meet with the future family during the pregnancy?" Sarah asked.

"No, Sarah," the nun replied, weeping.

"I'm sorry, Sister. I didn't intend to upset you, but you see, I too was one of those children who immediately found themselves, like George, in an orphanage—not with some family waiting for me with open and loving arms." Sarah now showed signs of lament.

"I know, I know, and I'm sorry. They didn't tell us that would happen, and until George came here several years ago, I didn't know." She paused, letting her emotions catch up with the commentary. "At the time, we—myself and the others involved—believed we were helping the religion by providing more Catholic children to worthy families. They played upon our feminine instinct to fulfill our motherhood destiny."

"And you seem today, through your candidness and your straightforward answers, to have questioned the entire procedure," Sarah continued.

"Yes. Again, until George showed up on my doorstep several years ago, I never questioned the motive for the births. After George told his fateful story and said he had identified me as his mother, I was sickened and distraught. At first, I had a hard time believing the entire story, but then I came to accept it. I had to ease my conscience by finding out what was going on. I feel horrible for George, but what can I do about it now? I was a pawn, caught in a game that masters play. I think of George constantly and pray for him daily. I hope someday to be able to repay him for all the damage I have done to his life."

Looking Sister Mary Theresa directly in the eye, Sarah said, "I know that George has some issues with this situation, as do I. And I know that he has, according to him, lost his faith. But I firmly believe that some kind of contact from you could go a long way in restoring his faith, particularly if you tell him what you have told me," Sarah said.

"By the way, Sister, your son told me that you have a biological sister who is also a member of the clergy. According to genome information, she is my mother. What is her name? Is she also a member of your convent in Provence?" Sarah pried, hoping the answer would be yes.

The pain in Sister Mary Theresa's eyes was evident as she hesitated to respond. She excused herself, got up from her desk, and walked over to the cross on the wall. She genuflected and knelt, uttering something Sarah could not understand.

A few minutes later, she returned.

"I'm sorry for the interruption to our conversation, but you overwhelmed me with your question. I don't know if my answer to your question is going to help you in your search; however, my biological sister's name was Sister Joan, and she was of the same order," Sister Mary Theresa began.

"Sister, you are speaking in the past tense. Are you implying that Sister Joan, my mother, is deceased?" Sarah's demeanor indicated deep depression.

"Unfortunately, yes, my dear," came the attempted consoling response of a biological aunt. "She died shortly after childbirth more than twenty-eight years ago."

R. W. Kay

Recomposing herself from the shock of her mother's demise, as her death was attributed to her birth, Sarah asked, "What was she like?"

"Well, for starters, she would have been a good mother. I say this because, knowing her death to be imminent, she refused to give you up. She put up such a battle the hospital acquiesced, permitting her to keep you and nurse you until her death.

"As for a sibling, she was a good sister, exceedingly kind, compassionate, and always worried about her little sister's well-being. We both started as nuns back in the States more than thirty plus years ago. We both received an opportunity to work in Rome, and we decided to expand our horizons, see other parts of the world. So we jumped at the chance to serve while seeing parts of the world. Ironically, we were both transferred to the Shrine of Mary Magdalene at the same time. She passed here, and she lies at the foot of the stairs leading up to the grotto. If you would like, I can take you there. I stop there myself every morning to say hello."

The two talked about family relationships, especially those remaining in the States and how Sarah's and George's trees intersected. From the conversation, Sister Theresa gained an understanding of her son's hurt and an appreciation of Sarah's family resemblance.

On the way to her mother's grave, Sarah had one last nagging question she had to ask. "What were they trying to do with all these surrogate mothers if it wasn't, as you were to believe, providing children to Catholic families in need?"

"I'm afraid I can't answer that with firsthand knowledge. I did some time ago do a little research, which led me to an archeologist by the name of D. Behlke here in Provence who did an abundance of work in the Holy Land."

"Why would he know the answer to such a unique question as that?"

"I don't know. I met him at an art exhibit in town, and we struck up one of those relationships where you feel free to confide in one another, and I did," Theresa unapologetically stated.

"And what did Mr. Behlke say?"

"He told me that among other things going on over there, there is a mad rush to discover relics of buried individuals; they're searching for bones that may provide enough microbial deposits to possibly clone the buried individual," Sister Theresa said quietly. "He went on to tell me that there's a real rush to find the relics of Jesus for, as he said, obvious reasons."

"And what would those be?" Sarah naively asked.

"So that Jesus is reincarnated from his DNA. Interesting, isn't it?" Theresa continued.

"Do you think that's what they were trying to accomplish with you and my mother? Bring somebody like Jesus back?" Sarah, aware of ribonucleic acid and deoxyribonucleic acid's possibilities in the life progeny theory, was having difficulty understanding this left-field explanation.

"I don't know, Sarah. I don't know. I do know that if you, like I, believe in some of the stories of Mary Magdalene, there's a good chance that Jesus is buried somewhere here in Southern France, so they will never find any trace of him in the Holy Land.

"If you get the opportunity, go down to Aux-en-Province and look Dr. David Behlke up. He might be able to give you more and better information than I can," Sister Mary Theresa said at the termination of their meeting.

"I will, Sister, and thank you for your information and our family togetherness. It has been a great pleasure meeting you."

They hugged and then turned and walked away. That was the last time the two would meet.

7

The next afternoon, Sarah placed a call to New York. It was midafternoon in Provence and early morning in New York. The call made to the DANNAR Corporation was directed toward her old friend Jayne.

"Well, hello stranger. How are you doing? It's been only a couple of weeks, and you miss me already?" Jayne gushed at the fact that Sarah was calling her from France.

"Fine, Jayne, just fine," Sarah responded. "I was thinking about calling you yesterday when something came up that I need your expert opinion or advice on."

"That's a new one, a PhD wanting the advice of a modest tech. You must be desperate. What can I do for you?"

Sarah spent the next half hour filling Jayne in on what had transpired over the last several days. She mainly dwelled on the story of the two sisters who had become pregnant.

"Jayne," Sarah continued, "this is something very special to me, confidential and for your ears only."

"Sounds intriguing. So what do you want to know?" Jayne responded, wanting to help her friend.

"My question to you, Jayne, is has DANNAR been involved in gene splicing or, better, determining male and female aspects of genes, DNA, or RNA in an attempt to utilize one or the other for procreation purposes?"

"Wow," Jayne responded. "That's some question you just asked. If I recall correctly, we sort of covered this subject the night of your going-away party, at least to some extent."

"Yes, Jayne, but I need an answer on this," Sarah pleaded. "Is it possible to dissect the male and female portions of DNA or RNA and segregate them such that they may be used to recreate or clone an individual, exclusive of one of their parents?"

"Yes, it is!" Jayne said. "The DANNAR corporation has been on the cutting edge of such a program for quite some time. We were on the verge of making that discovery, the replication module, long before the cloning of that sheep called Dolly in Scotland.

"And one other thing to keep in mind," Jayne said, sounding like a college professor. "Cloning is one thing; replication is something else entirely. If you clone someone, you get the results of the mother's and father's female and male genes. If you replicate an individual by extracting the male genes, DNA, or RNA from the replicants' offspring, you end up with a correct version of the individual you are attempting to create. Do you remember several years back the book called *The Boys from Brazil*?" Jayne asked. "It was a detective-type thriller."

"No, I must have missed that one. Why?"

"Because," Jayne began, "the storyline of that book was well on target, just ahead of its time concerning cloning of specific people."

"Who was cloned?" Sarah's interest was heightened.

"An attempt was made to clone Adolph Hitler, and in doing so, they made about twenty or so duplications, hoping one would be the reincarnation of the beast that killed millions of people. They reckoned that aside from just cloning the individual, nature was crucial to his development and nurturing. Hence, they sought to put the cloned children in homes around the world that resembled those where Hitler spent his childhood. The potential for one of the clones to reach maturity was cut short by the story's end. But the procedure was never right from the beginning. Cloning is not the same as replication, which is what DANNAR has been experimenting with over the years."

"Do you remember the Dolly cloning accomplishment?" Sarah sought a quick refresher course in cloning.

"I do, and in fact, I have an article here in my drawer somewhere. Hold on and let me find it." Jayne, the ever-present reference expert, saved anything and everything related to DANNAR's work.

"Yes, Sarah, I do have that information tucked away. This report came from the A&E Television Network and is written by the History.com editors. So there, I have done my due diligence in ensuring they cannot get me, or us, for plagiarizing. So here is what it says:

> The cells had been taken from the udder of a six-year-old ewe and
> cultured in a lab using microscopic needles, in a method first used

in human fertility treatments in the 1970s. After producing a few normal eggs, scientists implanted them into surrogate ewes; 148 days later one of them gave birth to Dolly.

Dolly's birth was announced publicly in February 1997 to a storm of controversy. On one hand, supporters argued that cloning technology can lead to crucial advances in medicine, citing the production of genetically modified animals to be organ donors for humans as well as "therapeutic" cloning, or the process of cloning embryos to collect stem cells for use in the development of treatments for degenerative nerve diseases such as Alzheimer's and Parkinson's. Some scientists also looked at animal cloning as a possible way to preserve endangered species. On the other hand, detractors saw the new cloning technology as potentially unsafe and unethical, especially when it was applied to what many saw as the logical next step: human cloning.

"Now for your sixty-four-thousand-dollar question regarding gene splicing," Jayne continued, now on a roll, gushing with information. "My good friend, whose name I can't mention, has told me that your identified procedure, replication, not cloning, has been accomplished many times within the last thirty years. Before you ask, Sarah, there are people out there who are actually replications of someone from the past."

"Are you serious, Jayne?" Sarah said with a great degree of skepticism, thinking that maybe Jayne was pulling her leg. "Is that possible?"

"Of course, it's true!" Jayne continued. "Technical advances have made it cheap and efficient to sequence the entire genome of humans who have lived tens of millennia ago. And the genetic information is startlingly complete. It provides everything from hair and eye color to an ability to determine allergies. It can be determined from a thousandth of an ounce of bone or tooth, and, like your Twenty-Three and Me test, the results reveal clues to the identities and origins of your ancestors.

"So, yes it is, according to a few of our scientists who have firsthand knowledge. They told me that it's already in use. The concept of cafeteria-selected children is a possibility based upon that concept."

"So you're telling me that DANNAR can split the male from the female portions of DNA, implant the male portion into a neutral female egg, and ultimately bear a child having the exact makeup of their father, or mother if that be the case," Sarah said, incredulous.

"Well, yes, more the father than the mother. That's because of the problem of the egg and the necessity for male genes to fertilize—as opposed to an egg in an egg, where fertilization at this point is unlikely. One more thing in this replication process: if the egg is not completely neutered and still has its DNA completely or partially remaining, an intended male offspring could be female. In other words, if you had the male genome of Christ, that has to be obtained through his offspring, assuming one exists, the replication, or the second coming, may turn out to be a woman. Wouldn't that make the cult of Mary Magdalene happy?" Jayne laughed.

"You may think this is funny, but these people are dead serious," Sarah replied, knowing the replication process was probably the catalyst propelling her inquisitive journey.

"It seems to me," Jayne said, launching into her final assessment, "that in the scenario you have outlined, there are only three possible outcomes, two of which spell the potential for disaster."

"And what do you mean three outcomes?" Sarah asked.

"Well, Sarah, let's assume that whoever—the pope, the College of Cardinals, or some rogue group within the Vatican walls—had the means. If they were able to implant the DNA of the Christ side of the family, excluding the Virgin Mary's, there could only be three potential outcomes, two of which seem rather strange to me.

"If we assume someone was able to obtain DNA from a child allegedly belonging to Jesus and Mary Magdalene, they could then isolate the Jesus gene, implant that into a neutral egg, implant a viable embryo into a surrogate, and ultimately, assuming all goes well during the gestation period, produce a child. That child, made with no mistake in the system, would be the replication of Jesus Christ.

"The other two alternatives," Jayne continued, "come from my understanding of Matthew, Mark, Luke, and John. The Bible implies that the Virgin Mary, Jesus's mother, was impregnated by the Holy Ghost. If that is the case, then the offspring would be the Holy Ghost. I suppose you might be able to consider that, as Jesus and the Holy Ghost are all the same, God. But if that works, you have to consider the concept as incest. That spells disaster for the Bible, the church, and all believers.

"The other alternative, and this could be the worst for the Christian religion, is that Christ was merely mortal in that there is someone else in the woodpile. It seems the latter could bring down the foundation of the Christian religion," Jayne concluded.

Of course, it would, Sarah thought. *That's probably the reason for discarding people like George and me; we're not related to Christ but, moreover, probably the individual in the woodpile.*

After a brief pause, Jayne again drew a valid conclusion. "It would seem whoever is doing this hasn't got it completely correct. Because of the present ineptitude, they haven't obtained the desired outcome; a female offspring could develop. No, depending upon your definition of recreation or procreation, a female offspring could be Christ. Just think," Jayne went on, "you, Sarah Birch, could be the Savior. Isn't it about time a woman assumes a position of parochial leadership? I'm sure the cult of Mary Magdalene would agree."

The parties conversed for another thirty minutes, laughing at the possibilities Jayne had just enumerated.

At the end of the conversation, they bid their adieus, and Sarah agreed to contact Jayne with further information as it came to light. Jayne decided to look further into DANNAR's secret project.

"Don't get yourself into trouble, Jayne. Be careful," Sarah admonished.

"I told you before," Jayne said, "I'm too old to care. Don't worry about me."

8

Sister Mary Theresa had mentioned an archeologist is living in Provence who was familiar with the constant search for human relics in the Holy Land. Sarah decided to visit his offices in the downtown of Aix-en-Provence.

After leaving the villa, Sarah asked Sister Josephine, the petite nun behind the front desk, to call a cab to take her to Aix-en-Provence.

"Oh, Miss Birch, you do know how far that is, don't you?" Sister Jo questioned.

"It's just down the hill from here, isn't it?" Sarah responded, looking inquisitively at the soon-to-be sister.

"Oh no," replied the nun. "It's almost back to Marseilles, where you came from a few days ago."

"That far?" Sarah looked at Sister Jo as if hoping she was wrong.

"Well, not quite as far as Marseilles, which is one hour, but about forty minutes from here, depending on who we get as a driver." She laughed.

"All right then. Make sure you get the fastest driver," Sarah responded as she, too, laughed.

Thirty minutes later, a driver in an old Ford truck pulled up in front of the hostelry. The driver honked as if he was late for his funeral.

"Hush," Sister Josephine warned. "Do you want Sister Mary Theresa to know you're out here making all this noise?"

Sarah stood in the doorway, watching the look on the driver's face when Sister Josephine mentioned Mary Theresa's name.

"Now, Miss Birch, what is the street number where you wish to go in Aix-en-Provence? I will tell Phillippe here, and he will take you there. Oh, yes, he does not speak a word of English. You may have to communicate using sign language."

Great, Sarah thought. "I wonder if he knows anything about Mary Magdalene he can share."

"Don't be silly." The young nun laughed. "Mary Magdalene. Now what was the address in Aux?"

"It's fifteen Cours Mirabeau," she answered as she sat in the shotgun seat of the ancient relic.

"Have a nice trip," was the last thing she heard voice wise until reaching Cours Mirabeau.

The building at 15 Cours Mirabeau looked as deserted as Christ's tomb after the resurrection and not as clean. The shades covering the windows and door were musty looking, like something out of the movie *Casa Blanca*, and she felt sure that when she attempted to open the door, the shades would disintegrate.

Of course, none of that happened. But what happened next was unexpected. Expecting to meet a wily, old, desert-wrinkled individual, she was mildly surprised when Dave Behlke came from behind a curtain where he had been dusting relics from one of his many digs.

"Hello," he said as he approached her from behind.

Doing a quick about-face, Sarah was stunned when Dr. Behlke appeared younger than she was.

"Well, hello," Sarah replied, incapable of any other reply, given the handsome individual standing before her. "My name is Sarah, Sarah Birch," she said before Dr. Behlke took over the conversation, enthralled by the devastatingly beautiful, raven-haired woman Sarah Birch was.

"Oh yes, Sarah," he said as he tripped on a chisel he had left on the floor. "Sarah, yes," he said a second time. "Sister Mary Theresa said you might be paying a visit sometime this week. So, Sarah, to what do I owe this wonderful chance meeting?" he gushed, letting the apparent attraction flow from his eyes to her beautiful face, slowly taking in the curvature of her Venus di Milo bodice.

With the typical abruptness of United States political correctness, Sarah would have called him out for his boldness and somewhat surly mannerism, but this was different. It felt good.

"So," Dave continued, his eyes incapable of leaving Sarah's face, "how can I help you?"

"I'm sure a million ways," Sarah responded, leaving the door open as her double entendre registered with Dr. Behlke.

"Well." Behlke smiled. "Let's start with the most perplexing and work our way to those where some commonality exists." He winked.

"That's a deal," Sarah responded and proceeded to put forth her question. The others would wait for a more advantageous time.

"Can you shed a little light on all these different stories I seem to be uncovering about the crucifixion of Christ and the activities that happened afterward?"

"I presume you are asking about Mary Magdalene and some of the stories about her and Jesus. Is that where this is going?"

"Yes, you are going to think me such a fool, a PhD with only a grade school education in the resurrection and the events surrounding it."

"No, no, you would be surprised at the lack of knowledge exhibited by most people about that subject. Most folks, especially Catholics, believe that she was a repentant prostitute who Christ saved. And that is about the sum and substance of their knowledge."

"I guess I believe that. The only place I remember her name was in my third-grade catechism class at St. Joseph's. Other than that, we never spoke much of her. And now I come to Provence, and her name, statues, pictures are everywhere, and people are praying to her."

"There have been many misrepresentations in the account of this fascinating woman. The church is primarily responsible for that," Dr. Behlke began, assuming his pulpit place on a barstool in his office.

"You see," he went on, "historically, and principally in Gnostic writings, women's equality with men, in most aspects of life but particularly religion, was not questioned. The Gospels of Mathew, Mark, Luke, and John show Mary Magdalene's importance to the Jesus story. As I'm sure you may recall, she was at the crucifixion of Jesus. In contrast, most others had departed. After helping to remove Jesus from the cross, she was the first to witness the resurrection, which in Gnostic biblical lore earned her the title of apostle to the apostles. If this story happened today, she would be the single most important person besides Jesus in the greatest story ever told.

"However, as I said, there have been many falsifications and juxtapositions in this story. For example, at the Council of Nicaea in 325, with three hundred eighteen Christian bishops, priests, and aides, significant decisions were made as to how the church would operate the religion's future. A vote was cast as to which Gospels to include in the New Testament and which doctrines were to be the guiding principles of the new Roman Church. This, almost three hundred years after the death of Christ, before any movement was made to galvanize the religion. And then it was done by a council of men. As a result, women were stripped of the place they had attained in the first three hundred years. You see, Sarah, for almost three hundred years, the early church consisted of women bishops and priests. With a swoop of the pen at Nicaea, women were denied their rightful place within Roman Catholicism."

"So," Sarah interrupted, "the church, as you described it, was not antiwoman from its beginning but primarily after the Council of Nicaea. Is that right?"

"Sort of, yes," Behlke responded. "But there were some detractors before Nicaea. For example, Timothy had something to say about women. He believed they should not be apostolic. Sarah, could you reach behind you and hand me one of those Bibles?"

"Anyone in particular? It seems you have a large number. Any particular version?" Sarah asked, noting his complete biblical library had more than thirty English translations, not including those in Hebrew, Greek, and Arabic.

"Any English version is OK. They're all generally consistent. Only occasionally do you get some far-out interpretation." He smiled, watching Sarah's eyes to determine if her return smile was fake or legitimate, believing an honest smile might mean some interest in him

After browsing through the pages of the biblical text, he stopped. Turning to his new student, he said, "Oh yes, here it is. This is what was placed in the Nicaean code as being acceptable. It comes from Timothy's first letter to Paul. It reads, 'Let a woman learn quietly with all submissiveness. I do not permit a woman to teach or to exercise authority over a man, rather, she is to remain quiet.'

"To add salt to the wound," Behlke continued, "two hundred sixty-six years later, a sermon given by Pope Gregory produced the idea that Mary Magdalene was a penitent prostitute, a disgraced and sinful person. This casting of Mary as a whore forever cast her as a marginal individual in the story, gelding the fact Mary Magdalene may have been one of the most important disciples in the biblical story.

"Mary Magdalene seemed to be an actual threat to the early Catholic Church, not only because she was a woman but also because for hundreds of years after the crucifixion, there were persistent rumors that Mary Magdalene was, in fact, the wife of Jesus," Behlke continued.

"So, you see, Sarah, if this fable about the marriage could exist, it would nullify the church's position on women. So, despite any supporting scriptural evidence to the contrary, the church tried to turn Mary Magdalene into a prostitute and succeeded, as your knowledge of the catechism sheds evidence.

"Unfortunately, it is obvious why Mary Magdalene has been rejected by history. The question is, does the church have the mettle to say that the Council of Nicaea was possibly wrong? At least the church recanted Gregory's faux pas. However, the story's legacy remains, even though in 1969, the identification of Mary Magdalene as the 'sinful woman' was removed from the General Roman calendar by Pope Paul VI."

"That's right. I remember that!" Sarah jokingly blurted.

"Of course you do," Behlke playfully responded. "Let us see." He looked over at her, his interest in Mary Magdalene now taking a back seat. "That should make you somewhere about seventy-one years old. You sure do wear your age well!"

The jovial playfulness and its obvious sexual overtones made Sarah blush with anticipation of what might come next. "I'd say, Herr Doctor, you left Mary Magdalene in a lurch while dallying with my emotions. That wasn't a very gentlemanly thing to do. Do you always treat your women that way?"

"No, no, of course not. It's just that no one as beautiful has ever walked through these doors and livened this old museum up the way you have," Dave shyly responded.

Behlke's apparent shyness was picked up immediately by Sarah, and she thought, *This is the kind of guy I've been seeking.* Then, as if time were standing still, she said, "But what about Mary Magdalene? What else were you going to say?"

Taken aback, he picked up exactly where he had left off. "Oh yes, Mary," he muttered. "Mary Magdalene is now considered to be a saint by the Catholic, the Eastern Orthodox, Anglican, and Lutheran Churches. In 2016, Pope Francis, on July 22, one thousand, four hundred and three years after her being branded a whore, made her birthday a Catholic feast day. Although something is slowly taking place to recognize this marvelous woman, the timing and past discrepancies are a sad commentary for the church."

"Thank you, Dr. Behlke, for that fine lecture. I haven't heard anything that thrilling since I left my years at Stanford," Sarah commented, giving him a well-rounded applause for his concern.

"A cardinal?" Dave responded. "You're a Stanford cardinal. I knew there was something I liked about you the minute I heard you shuffling on this dirty floor. Here in Aux-en-Provence, I meet this soul mate who now tells me she is also a Stanford cardinal. This calls for a celebration, and I know just the place. So, how about lunch?" Dave questioned, not wanting this beautiful quarry out of his sight.

"Oh, Doctor Behlke, I have already imposed upon your good nature," she began before being cut off by Dave.

"No, no, I insist. It's not often a fellow alum walks through my door and asks for information. I have a lot more to give you. My lecture is not complete. We still have some work to do." He smiled, almost childlike, hoping she would say yes to the invitation.

"Well, if you insist," she coyly replied.

"Wonderful!" Dave interjected, anxious for any overture providing an inkling of yes. "That settles it. Lunch is on me."

Lunch was a French delight for Sarah, as she had never experienced such details to perfection as the waiters and staff of the Le Jardin d'Amalula seemed to be. Everyone, including the busboys, was concerned that the meal was something more than just eating, more than just imbibing exquisite French wine; it was a gastronomic delight. Being a novice in the French eating dance, Sarah decided to sit back and allow Dave to order and interact with the restaurant personnel. His first assignment and her first lesson began when they entered the restaurant and the maître de approached the two.

"Bon jour, Monsieur Behlke," the maître de greeted them.

"Bon jour, Monsieur Phillipe," the greeting continued, and Sarah could only guess at what was said. It was, however, evident that Dave was no stranger to this establishment.

During lunch, the focus was on the food, and discussion of anything other than the accouterments associated with the meal was *verboten*, to use Dave's word.

After finishing the meal, kudos for the restaurant personnel were meted out, and the subject matter of Sarah's interest was immediately revisited.

"So, tell me, Sarah, what was the motivation behind the impregnation of several nuns and then disposing of the offspring at the moment of birth?" Dave questioned with a quizzical look of uncertainty.

"That's the big question, isn't it? I have no idea, only supposition based on my education and my work background. It anything I surmise a conspiracy theory, no better and no worse than most," Sarah replied.

Completely enamored with the vivacious young lady before him, Dave played along. "Ok, I'll bite. What's your conspiracy theory?"

"It's not a theory. It's just more of a gut feeling. Have you ever had one of those?" Sarah quizzed.

"Many times, in my business. Usually, they turn out to be worth more consideration than some of the hypotheses learned from the books." Behlke winked. "Go on, Doctor. I'm very interested to hear your thoughts."

"Are you familiar with the works of the DANNAR corporation?" Sarah asked, her presentation juices flowing as though it was the first day of class and she had been assigned the responsibility for the day's focus.

"No, I can't say I am. Should I be?" Dave questioned.

"Well, the name of the company might give you a hint as to what they work on. DANNAR stands for Deoxyribo-Neucleiciribo Acid and Ribo-Nucleic Acid, the building blocks of life."

"You medical MDs and PhDs are way ahead of we poor earth-digging archaeologists when it comes to these magical tricks of your trade. Can you be a little more specific?" Dave laughed while ordering another round of drinks for the two of them.

"All right, Doctor of archeology, here goes." Sarah snickered. "DNA, or deoxyribonucleic acid, is a self-replicating material present in nearly all living organisms. It's the main constituent of chromosomes. It's also the carrier of genetic information. DNA is the hereditary material in humans and almost all other organisms. Nearly every cell in a person's body has the same DNA. Most DNA is in the cell nucleus."

"And what is the other responsible for doing?" Dave was sincere in his questioning as he sipped his newest aperitif, a martini with three olives on the dirty side.

"RNA or ribonucleic acid is also present in all living cells. Its principal role is to act as a messenger carrying instructions from DNA. Together they represent life as we know it."

"OK, so what is this DANNAR company doing with its study?" Dave's uncertainty was growing while receiving a quick study of life. Despite some misgivings, he gave Sarah his undivided attention.

"According to a good friend of mine with the DANNAR corporation, the structure of DNA and RNA has been widely studied by DANNAR. Over the last forty years, it has been determined it can now be manipulated to replicate a deceased individual."

"And I suppose to do this, you would need to have some particular individual's remains where viable DNA and RNA can be captured. Correct?" asked Dave, now settling in for a more academic discussion.

"Well, not quite," Sarah said. "If you can replicate someone from their DNA, you might get a copy of one or both of their parents. But if you could find an offspring of an individual and then be able to segregate the male and female chromosomes, you could get an exact replication of the man or woman you were seeking."

"Replicate? You mean clone or copy, don't you? If I recall from my dissertation committee, replicating means the same," Behlke replied with a bit of skepticism.

"No, we are talking the same. Replicating provides the exact likeness of an individual replicated."

"Let me see if I understand what you are telling me. Suppose I were fortunate enough to find in my diggings the grave of Pharaoh Ramses and his family. And if we could extract DNA from his son or daughter, under the DANNAR Corporation's procedure, we could bring the Pharaoh Ramses back to life?"

"Yes, that is precisely what I am saying. I think somebody is looking to revive the Savior," Sarah said, coldly enough to send a shiver down her back and that of Dr. Behlke's.

"Preposterous!" Behlke blurted out, loud enough to draw the attention of other diners and the maître de.

"Is everything all right, Monsieur Behlke?" Phillipe said.

"Everything is fine, Phillipe. I apologize if I startled your customers," Dave responded, chuckling over his unexpected outburst. Turning to Sarah and still laughing, he said, "Go on with your conspiracy doctrine. You now have me completely mesmerized."

"As I started to say before you so rudely interrupted me," she said, laughing, "the DANNAR corporation has gone way beyond cloning. They have figured out a way to recreate an original human being by defining specifically the male or female DNA that made up the original person." Sarah continued outlining the procedures as best as she could.

Behlke sat, sipping his aperitif, listening attentively, and waiting for the piece de resistance, as the French call it, the Sarah theory.

"So, Sarah, where is this all leading?"

"Well, I believe that some group in the church has picked up on the DANNAR research and is trying to replicate an individual but hasn't yet found the precise individual they want."

"And who would that be?" Dave was perched on the edge of his chair.

"Well, because they discarded individuals of my age, they did not have the correct equation in place when my cousin and I were in the program. Since the time of Dolly's cloning and the Masters and Johnson groundbreaking studies, it is no longer necessary to have coitus to fertilize a woman. Nor is it necessary to have spermatozoa from the male to fertilize an egg. It can be obtained from the blood, or more to the point, from the DNA. Incidental to this entire procedure is the one constant, the woman. Now, would not any woman suffice? The answer to that is yes. Then," she continued as if on a mission to prove to her doctoral committee that her dissertation was the only accurate representation of the subject matter covered.

"Then," she repeated, "if any female would suffice, why do they pick young virgin nuns to be impregnated?"

"I have no idea whatsoever," Dave sheepishly replied, feeling a bit out of his comfort zone.

"A virgin is an absolute necessity," Sarah began before being cut off.

"Are you serious?" Behlke replied, half in a state of disbelief, while the other half dwelled on the pure revelation of the possibility. "This is beginning to sound a little unrealistic to me."

"You mean like some of the stories we have been led to believe since childhood?" Sarah set the stage for her next statement. "If you wanted to recreate Jesus, what would you need?" She smiled, looking David square in the eye.

"I suppose a woman," he began.

"What kind of woman?"

"A Middle Eastern woman," David replied.

"No, David. Come on. You can do better than that," she egged him on.

"I don't know," he said, steadfastly denying knowing the answer.

"What about a virgin?" Sarah asked.

"Oh, yes. I guess you would need that, wouldn't you?"

"What else, David? What else?" Sarah pressed.

"Well, if we use DANNAR's procedure, which was just recently explained to me, some DNA from a girl named Sarah, although I would prefer to keep it all to myself," he mused, noticing that his joke was not lost on her.

She smiled, aware of the implication in what the archeologist from Jerusalem just said.

"But, Sarah, where is this going? Do you have a hypothesis?"

"I do," Sarah reverently answered. "Just follow the yellow brick road, and it leads directly to Oz. I think this road leads to the possibility of the second coming of Christ."

9

Meanwhile, 203 miles away in the Italian town of Genoa, Italy, five members of the Society of the Christian Brotherhood were in a closed-door meeting with several lay members of the Church of St. Mathew. The conversation was the high cost their order was absorbing by doing business with the DANNAR corporation.

Father Anselmo Brugundini, a man in his mid to late fifties, headed a group that believed medical improvements would ultimately hasten the latter portions of the New Testament predictions.

"Father Anselmo, you must recognize that we cannot guarantee you the replication of the individual you seek if you continually provide us with faulty input. The samples you took from under St. Peter's of the apostle Peter proved faulty, as have so many others you have provided over the years, obtained from your digs in Jerusalem."

"But, Mr. Hill, we have followed your instructions to the letter," the priest indignantly replied.

"That is true to a degree, Father," Hill responded while attempting to keep his composure. "For some reason, you do not understand that cloning and replication are two completely different processes that will provide different outcomes."

"You are right. I don't understand, and neither do any of the others gathered here today," Father Anselmo replied after observing the blank stares on the faces of the members at the meeting. "In every instance of viable samples provided from some of our holiest relics, we continually are advised by your researchers nine months later that conception was accomplished, but the outcome was something—or should I say *someone*—other than expected. And three times, St. Peter turned out to be female. Your system is flawed, and we are no longer of the belief that our expenditures are achieving any positive results."

"But—" Hill attempted to respond.

"Over the past thirty years, we have spent over two hundred ninety-seven million euros on a project your company has developed and prospered. Yet here we are, once again without any possible results that are worth considering."

"I understand your concern, Father. And as a Christian and Catholic myself, I am shocked by the outcomes. However, at last year's meeting with you and the distinguished members present, our scientists tried to explain the replication issue's new parameters. And the consensus was that the new approach was blasphemous to Christian teachings and thus could not and would not be permitted."

"That is correct and still is true," the priest said.

"Just think for a moment how many different stories exist about the Savior and His relationship with Mary Magdalene," Hill commenced.

"Here you go again, pushing something that just didn't happen," the priest immediately responded.

"But, Father, Christ was never a Christian. He was a Jew Essene and, as such, subscribed to both Jewish tradition and law. And, Father, that same law said that all rabbis of that age should be married. If that's the case, isn't it probable and possible that he was married and may have had one or more offspring, as many Gnostics have written?"

"Of course, anything is possible. However, that is not our belief," Father Anselmo responded.

"It is not mine either, Father, but as a scientist and an educator such as yourself, along with your learned colleagues, can you afford to turn a deaf ear to this possibility?" Hill reasoned. "The stakes are too high, and as you have invested yourself so deeply in this project, isn't it better you than someone else crack this egg. Because our ear to the floor tells us others are attempting this very revival."

"Who else but we are searching for Christ?" a member of the group listening to the speakerphone conversation blurted out.

"Well," Hill said, shuffling some papers, a noise heard on the other end of the phone line. "From the information obtained by our investigative department, it seems two other companies are working on similar projects, though not as successful as ours."

"Successful!" one of the attendees called out. "You call thirty years without the results we anticipated we would receive successful?"

"No, I wouldn't," Hill backtracked. "But you are a lot closer than they are to reaching your mutual goals."

"And who are these individuals or groups?" Father Anselmo probed.

Hill reflected on his response, drawing upon his sales role to say what would bring the Society of the Christian Brotherhood back into the fold.

"Well, gentlemen, the first group is a Muslim group intent on following their Qur'an, which tells that neither the resurrection nor the ascension happened. If they can replicate Christ, they believe they can destroy Christianity."

"That's interesting," Father Anselmo replied. "And how far along are they in their attempt to duplicate Christ?"

"Nowhere near the possibility you have if you would try to think out of the box and look at the possibility that Christ might have sired a child."

"Yeah, OK. Who is the other group?"

"A group of disaffected Protestants who would like to do nothing less than destroy the Catholic Church," came the immediate reply.

"And are they American or European Protestants, and how well financed are they?" someone called out from the group.

"That is hard to say. However, the information received indicates the group is of European origin."

"That figures," a priest named Father Bartholomew said.

"So, we are now in a race to find the Savior to save the religion that honors him," Father Anselmo said to his group membership. "Isn't the twenty-first century wonderful!"

While the group members sat silenced by this new turn of events, Jim Hill seized the opportunity to once again explain to them the rudiments of the DANNAR corporation's program to bring back to life the original version of someone who had died centuries ago.

"If it's Christ you're seeking, you are going to have to change your thinking about the ascension and start thinking like some of your French and Spanish counterparts who believe Christ took Mary Magdalene as his wife and sired a daughter named Sarah. If Sarah is Christ's blood child, she would be the linchpin we need to obtain a DNA sample. Not some of these remains from Jerusalem you keep supplying. Who knows who they are. Up to this point, Father, over the past thirty years, you have produced a total of three hundred and twenty children, none of whom seem to be apostles or Jesus Himself."

"So, Mr. Hill, are you suggesting we move our focus from Jerusalem to ..." He hesitated. "Provence, France, and start digging there?" Father Anselmo asked, showing signs of disappointment and frustration.

"Father and gentlemen, if Christ, did or didn't die on the cross but did have a child with Mary Magdalene, that child could very well be buried in Provence, France. One iota of DNA from her remains could or would be the beginning of a possible regeneration of your religion. I would suggest you consider the alternatives of not pursuing this adventure further," Hill proposed.

"Thank you for your sage advice, Dr. Hill. We shall take it under consideration and think about your proposal. Thank you for attending our meeting via telephone this morning. We will contact you if necessary. Goodbye." Father Anselmo abruptly ended the conversation.

10

Sarah woke early. Eager thoughts about again spending the day with Dave sent shivers and goose bumps throughout her body; she was smitten with him. She had read from many of the day's romance novels that this was the way it worked. Many stories espoused the beauty of love at first glance, and here it was a distinct reality. Her educational background belied the experience, but there it was, something that went beyond rational thinking. Never in her twenty-nine years of life had she ever experienced such euphoria, such joy, such rapture. It was as if her senses had left her, yet here she was, a stranger in a strange land, experiencing new customs, new food, new ways of thinking about things, and now feeling the exhilaration of being in love.

I wonder if this is the way Mary Magdalene felt so many years ago when she sat at Christ's feet, Sarah thought as she found more and more kindred feelings toward the patron Saint of Provence.

A few minutes later, the telephone rang.

"Hello," she cooed, knowing the call would have to be from David.

"Good morning, sunshine. Did you have a good night's sleep?"

"Well, I couldn't stop thinking about Mary Magdalene and her involvement with Jesus," she lied, knowing the entire night's tossing, turning, and hugging of her pillow was due entirely to him.

"Oh well," he responded, feeling rejected, "I hoped you might have been thinking of me."

"Well," she began, not sure of what to say, not knowing if she should allow her feelings to be known. The orphanage had not prepared her for this beautiful, enigmatic feeling. *What to do? What to say?*

"Of course, some of it was," she said, not wanting to lose the moment. "How could I not think of that wonderful lunch and the sumptuous dinner you introduced me to? You know, Provence is a wonderful place," she said to give her more time to think about how to let him know but not allow him to see that she was very interested in the archaeologist of Jerusalem.

"I'm so glad you enjoyed it," came a less than enthusiastic reply.

Feeling as if she had understated her original contractional opener, Sarah switched to a more aggressive position. "Would you like to do something today?"

"Of course," came David's jubilant answer. "I thought we might see some of Provence this morning, catch lunch, and then later this afternoon, I would introduce you to Father Jacques Cronin, the pastor of Eglise Saint Joan. He can give you a different perspective of what may have happened two thousand years ago."

All the while David was talking, Sarah's mind was wandering unconsciously without registering anything said—that is, other than the talk of lunch. She looked forward to a second of David's gastronomic lunches, especially with a man who kept her intrigued, a man who treated her the way the romance novels said it should be done. This was done without asking for anything in return except for her presence. She was someone he could find enough time to share. *Is this the way love works?* she thought. *Could this be the real thing? Is this the way it works? The feeling of electricity surging through every vein in your body, a desire to touch the man, to gobble him up, to feel his hands on mine, his warm breath on my neck.*

"Is that OK, Sarah," David asked, not knowing if she was still on the other end of the line.

"Yes, yes," she responded, almost unable to control the feelings that came from just talking with David. "I'll be ready in forty-five minutes."

"Good. I'll meet you in front of the hotel."

"That's a deal. See you in forty-five," Sarah responded with a smile as broad as Fifth Avenue.

It seemed as though Bob Fossi had choreographed her entrance. Sarah came through the hotel's revolving door precisely forty-five minutes later. Her dress was captivating, and the look it inspired was not lost on the archaeologist from Jerusalem.

"My gosh," David said. "My gosh, you are going to outshine the tourist crowd. You look ravishing."

"Thank you, Dave. It's only something I found in my bag," Sarah said, knowing full well that she had purchased the outfit in the hotel earlier that morning.

"Well, wherever you found it, it's a prodigious start to our sightseeing tour of some of Provence. I hope you will enjoy it."

Sarah knew full well that a trip around the block with David would be more than well worth it. This experience might be something she had sought her entire life, with someone of her own.

"Now that you're in the car, I have a unique surprise for you," he said as he pulled out a pair of earphones from the glove compartment. "We're going to take a whirlwind trip through the streets of Provence, and you'll get the flavor of the town by a prerecorded message I made last night after I left you."

"OK," Sarah said with the enthusiasm of a child getting her first toy.

"One more thing. I plan on taking you through some of the romantic areas like the beautiful lavender fields, where we can take our wine and cheese and have a splendid picnic."

"David, that sounds wonderful. Let's get started. I can't wait for the lavender fields," she uttered, not realizing that she was showing her emotions toward the romanticism that David had announced. She immediately positioned the bulky hearing device on her head as David set the controls so that the volume was appropriate.

Sarah was appreciative for two reasons. The first was the volume, and the second was the ability to withdraw a little from a possible faux pax she had made, thinking but not knowing if he felt the same way.

After a little crackling, David's voice came on, and it was apparent he was reading a script from the local chamber of commerce.

"Famed for its waters and its art, Aix-en-Provence wears its dual identity well, from refreshing fountains to old buildings harking back to past splendors, from the buzz of markets and lively café terraces to the International Lyric Art Festival. Proud of its exceptional heritage, Aix champions all forms of art and learning, and its refined way of life has an instant appeal. With the new trappings of a city embracing its transformation, it seamlessly combines its many facets

"Enjoying wine, French bread, and cheese in France must be any food lover's dream. Add dreamy villages and endless fields of fragrant flowers to the mix, and you get the ultimate layback, romantic day in Provence! I hope you enjoyed the ride. I know I have, and the scenery of Provence is much more splendid since you came into that dusty archaeologist's office and life."

What do with a statement like that? This was what she had waited to hear, but now, what to do? *How do I respond?* she thought.

A quick turn of the driver's wheel answered her question as David reached over to hold her back from moving forward in the event she had failed to buckle her seat belt. As his hand came along, she reached out and grabbed it, squeezing it as if letting go would ruin the moment.

Instinct caused David to reduce the speed, and he looked over at Sarah and leaned toward her to feel her sensual lips demanding to be kissed. Despite the fact that the car was moving forward at a relatively swift rate, their lips met.

With the car now swerving on a well-used highway, David slammed on the brakes, his lips still locked impetuously on hers. The car skidded to a stop, but the osculating continued, each sending their tongues deeper and deeper into the other.

"Oh my God, I can't believe this is happening," David said, his breath leaving him, being replaced by a panting regulated by the pounding of his heart.

"Me neither, but let's not stop," Sarah replied, totally out of character.

That was all the encouragement needed; a portion of the afternoon was on a highway, somewhere in France between the city of Aix-en-Provence and the lavender fields.

Regaining their composure after a time of intense necking and petting, as the old-timers called it, David abruptly said, "It's time to head to the lavender fields where love abounds, and you, Sarah, are going to experience a romanticism only be in the country noted for romance.

"Wonderful," Sarah replied while attempting to remove splotches of lipstick from his white shirt collar. However, no matter how hard she tried, success was unattainable.

"You know, David, we have to get that lipstick off your shirt before we meet with your priest friend."

"Not to worry. I plan to make the other side of my shirt look the same way once we get to the lavender fields and can find our little hideaway."

"Oh, you do, do you? And what makes you think I'll go along with your little scheme?" she joked, a little concerned about how far he thought he was going to take this interlude in the fields of lavender.

One location in June was not necessary, as the countryside abounded in the color and fragrance of lavender. And it was a surety that David had a hideaway nestled somewhere within the vast sea of purple. Driving down a dusty country lane, they finally arrived at a location where the lavender met the blue of a lake and the mountains' granite color.

"This is beautiful," Sarah exclaimed. "Do you come here often?" she questioned, concerned that this locale might be his love affair rendezvous point and that this was not his first rodeo.

"Not as often as I would like," he replied, leaving Sarah wanting to know if she was the first to visit his hallowed ground.

"No, I found this spot several years ago, and I come out here whenever the world becomes too much for me. I guess you might say this is my little piece of heaven." David laughed.

"And have you brought others here to your temple of love?" Sarah probed, desperately wanting to know he was not like the university males who had replaced shaking hands with a jump in the hay, something she detested about her generation's attitude toward sex.

"No, Sarah. You are the only one who has been here. The location is where I meditate, so there is no room for someone else. Except for you."

The morning passed quickly, and David set lunch on a red-and-white checkered cloth, the main course being French bread, Camembert cheese, walnuts, fresh fruits, and, of course, several bottles of Burgundy wine.

The beginning of the afternoon was a remake of the earlier version of love experienced in the car, only this time on a blanket David had laid among the lavender fields.

On the trip back to Aix-en-Provence, the hand holding and gestures of two people in love continued. When they finally arrived back in town, they agreed that each had better clean up, eliminating any traces of the morning's affair.

11

Several hours after leaving the lavender fields, David arrived for a second time at the hotel where Sarah was staying. Each had meticulously changed their clothes and dusted themselves off with the cologne in their repertoire, eliminating any indication of their morning activities.

After driving to the Eglise Sant Joan, Sarah was mildly surprised to see the cathedral. The twin spires rose majestically to the sky.

"Is this where Father Jacques makes his home? What is he, some sort of bishop or something?" Sarah questioned, her eyes admiring the grandeur of the vestibule as David pulled the massive wooden doors open.

"No, not a bishop, just a good guy. I think you're going to like him," David replied as the giant doors slammed shut behind them.

Entering the nave, an older, well-manicured priest was in the process of genuflecting before the altar. After arising in what appeared to be a problematic exercise, he turned and welcomed the visitors.

He smiled, his blue eyes twinkling in the afternoon haze of the church's interior. "And this must be Sarah, our American visitor who wants to know about Mary Magdalene," he said to David, then turned to Sarah. "I've heard so much about you in a short time. David here seems to know a great deal about you and the questions you have. I don't know if he told you, but he, with his knowledge obtained in Jerusalem, may know more about this subject than I." Father Jacques smiled while winking at Sarah.

After the introductions were completed, Father Jacques wanted to hear from Sarah her concerns about the Mary Magdalene story and what she was seeking in Provence, France.

"But before you get too uncomfortable in this hard pew, why don't we go over to the rectory where the atmosphere and the accouterments are a little kinder to our behinds." Father Jacques laughed.

Upon their arrival, Sarah explained her reason for being in Provence, her story leading to her conspiracy theory and her growing interest in the Mary Magdalene story.

"I can say I don't find that difficult to believe. There has been a belief for years that there is a Jesus bloodline in Europe, and now with the advantages derived from modern medicine and scientific advances, I'm sure the search will intensify.

"But I must warn you to be incredibly careful to whom you tell your story, and particularly your theory. There are many competing entities out there that would not want their research, or their real intent, to be known.

"And," he continued, assuming a profoundly severe look, "there are others who may believe your utterance to be the highest form of blasphemy."

"I find that hard to believe here in the twenty-first century," Sarah responded.

"It's true," Father Jacques snapped, using the spontaneous depiction to leave a lasting impression. "You must remember, this is not America, where you have First Amendment rights to say anything and everything you want. This is Europe where Christianity began, and some folks take maladjusted comments very seriously here. That is why, and I reiterate, be careful to whom you talk about this compassionate issue."

"I think, Father," David said to develop a more relaxed discussion, "Sara has a series of questions about the relationship of Jesus and Mary Magdalene and also questions relating to her conspiracy theory, as she just called it."

"Fine." said the priest. "Where would you like to start? Go ahead, Sarah. I can see you have something you want to ask."

"Yes, Father, I do, and I hope you will excuse me if I seem too forward."

"No, no, this has been a quasi-religious conversation, so all questions are fair," Father Jacques responded in his characteristically good nature. "Go ahead, Sarah, ask your questions."

"I think, Father, given my upbringing, these questions may be about more clarification about religion for me. Do you believe Jesus was the Savior?" she began her interrogation.

"Yes, I do," came the immediate response.

"But do you also believe he may be buried somewhere here in Provence?"

"Yes, I do," he responded.

"How is that possible? It conflicts with everything we have learned."

"That is true, but sometimes everything we learn is not true," the priest responded, raising his hands, gesturing *who knows*.

"So, is it also your belief that Jesus and Mary Magdalene were married and had a child?"

"I believe that Jesus and Mary Magdalene, along with several others, safely made their way to Southern France after a botched crucifixion by the Romans. And they had a child, and the holy one and his family consecrated our terra firma."

"Doesn't your view conflict with that of the Catholic belief?" Sarah asked.

"Yes, it does, but how do you know their beliefs are true? You have already seen misrepresentation of things that happened, and then they are eliminated from the Bible. Or how about the Council of Nicaea? Is that all correct? We already know the answer to that, don't we?

"Yes, there are some flaws in their beliefs. Let us just suppose for a moment that Jesus was not the Son of God but instead the Son of man as he proclaimed, a magnificent healer who carried this story way beyond its intended conclusion. Instead, let us also suppose he colluded with Mary Magdalene to concoct a story that he would die on the cross for humankind's sins, be resurrected, and ultimately ascend to heaven forty days later. Now, let us suppose this all came to pass, that his preaching is believed, and as a result, the Jewish community branded him as a false prophet and sought to have his head on a stick. Now, supposing further, during pillow talk with his wife, Mary Magdalene, he concocted a story and a ruse that she would be the first to witness the resurrection after his death. But something unforetold happened. He did not die on the cross. Instead, when Mary Magdalene and company brought him down, he was still alive. Rather than place him in the tomb provided by Joseph, they moved him elsewhere where he could be nursed back to life. Then on Easter Sunday, when the tomb was found open and missing, its occupant, Mary Magdalene, could announce the good news.

Now," Father Jacques continued, "let us also suppose that in the time following Jesus in his pale, disheveled, tired, and sick appearance, he appears to the group of apostles, giving them instruction to 'Go into the world and proclaim the Gospel to the whole creation.' But now along comes the Gospel of Mary, which augments this meeting. She says the apostles were scared and not familiar enough with Christ's teachings, and she reconciles them such that they follow Christ's orders, and shortly after that, the holy family sets sail for France."

"Is that what the Gospel of Mary says?" Sarah asked.

"No, not in that particular scenario, but she does console the apostles and is seen as the apostle of apostles from that easing of the apostles' fear," Father Jacques continued. "Now, isn't that story just as plausible, just as possible, just as probable as the other versions of the four chroniclers? Could this all have happened? And is it any less possible than the stories we find in the New Testament?

"As it was all written sixty or more years after it allegedly happened, it is unsubstantiated, and John, the last of the supposed chroniclers of the incident, seems to have plagiarized Matthew, Mark, and Luke and then embellished the story to ensure that Christ did die on the cross by inserting into the account that a soldier put a spear into Christ's side.

"That seems rather strange because the other three chroniclers, Matthew, Mark, and Luke, drew particular attention to the Roman guard in charge of the crucifixion. Each of them gives some account of his impression of the man on the cross.

"According to Matthew in 27:54, the guard said, 'Surely this man was the Son of God.' Almost to the tee in Mark 15:39, he said the same thing, while Luke used a little different phrasing, saying, 'Surely this was a righteous man.' Yet John has this same individual placing a spear in Christ's side. Most of John's writings are not in concert with the other chroniclers, and his works came last.

"So, you see, Sarah, there are a lot of conjectures and misrepresentations that force a person to decide for themselves what they believe and who they believe. Everything we read is pure conjecture, as in each instance of Christ's sightings, something is less than factual, or better yet, less than empirical or pragmatic. What we are left with is, as Thomas Aquinas labeled it, faith."

At that moment, the sound of breaking glass was heard from the anteroom. Based on the previous admonition given by Father Jacques, Sarah was quite jumpy.

"What was that?" Sarah's knee-jerk reaction to the silence breaker almost propelled her out of the chair.

"Oh, don't worry. It's only my housekeeper, Mrs. Pauget. She checks on me constantly." Then he called out, "Is everything all right in there, Mrs. Pauget?"

"Yes, sir, Father. I'm sorry if I interrupted you. I dropped a glass, and it broke. If it's all right, I will just clean it up and be out of here momentarily."

"That's fine, Mrs. Pauget. Take your time and be careful," the good priest responded lovingly.

Turning to his guests, the priest continued, "Forgive Mrs. Pauget. She is a harmless old woman who checks on me constantly. She listens to my telephone conversations, and if the truth be known"—he smiled—"she probably listens to the confessions of our parishioners. She's just a lonely, old woman, a person with no life of her own. You probably know the type."

Sarah forced another grin. "Yes, Father, of course, we all know of people like that."

"So yes," he began again, "I do have beliefs that are different from institutional Catholicism. We may never know who wrote the Gospel of John. It is apparent, however, that John's Gospel is fundamentally different from the others. The others are so alike in their Gospels they have come to be called the Synoptic Gospels, or Gospels that are characterized by comprehensiveness of views. In other words, they are congruent. John, however, does not include the same incidents, raising questions about the validity of his writings.

"What is known about our patron saint is becoming more and more rich with each passing day, thanks to the findings by archaeologists like David here. More and more digs in Jerusalem and other places in the Holy Land are turning up information that is changing the entire complexion of Western religion as we know it.

"Such is the case of our dear lady Mary Magdalene. It was only a short time ago in archeologists' time that the Gospel according to Mary (Magdalene) was uncovered. Of course, as a Gnostic document, it has little, if any, relevance for the Catholic Church. In the text, Mary is seen as a source of revelation, with knowledge of the teachings of Jesus since many of the apostles believe she maintained a closer relationship with Jesus than any of the apostles.

"In the text, Christ has charged the apostles to go forth and preach the good news to the Gentiles. But, for lack of understanding, they are afraid to go out among the Gentiles. Peter seeks out Mary to reveal to the apostles words they have not heard from Jesus. The rationale for this, according to Peter, is that Jesus loved her more than the other women. She provides the apostles with words allegedly coming straight from Christ. She reveals something contrary to Catholic teachings, that we are not a sinful lot but instead we are human, and as such, we need to look past our humanity and find true happiness.

"Christ then sends them to preach the good news to the Gentiles, and he leaves. The disciples are left sad, without confidence to fulfil their mission. Mary encourages them to carry on with what they have been asked to do.

"Peter asks Mary to communicate to the disciples the words they have not heard from Jesus, since they knew that Jesus 'loved her more than the rest of the women.' Mary talks about one of her visions, full of Gnostic connotations. Mary explains the difficulties the soul must overcome to reveal its true spiritual nature in ascending to its eternal resting place.

"Upon the termination of her vision, Andrew and Peter doubt her story. Peter then announces that he doubts the Lord preferred her to the other disciples. Levi, however, defends her and blames Peter for attacking Mary. He rebukes Peter, saying, 'You, Peter, have always been hot-tempered.' At that point, Levi encourages the disciples to accept that the Lord preferred Mary to themselves and invites them to go and preach the Gospel.

"This is, pretty much, all the information that could be gleaned from the fragmented texts of this Gospel. Certainly not much but enough to discern the attitude toward women in the new formative church."

"Why then, Father, is there so much pessimism about Mary Magdalene and Jesus possibly being married?" Sarah asked, feeling a loss for someone who had been dead for a couple thousand years.

"The reason for all this negativity about Mary Magdalene is that the proof for the historical marriage between Jesus of Nazareth and Mary Magdalene is difficult to find, if not intentionally deleted from biblical accounts. Just think how problematic it would have been for any of the four chroniclers to work around such an observation," Father Jacques opined with his persistent argument.

"It is overwhelming trying to find issues that identify a marriage, but no one seems to want to question Jesus's celibacy. The only thing that continues to argue for Jesus's celibacy is two thousand years of unrelenting theological bullying.

"Unfortunately, Sarah, there is no definitive ability to determine if Christ and Mary Magdalene were married. At this point, it is only conjecture. However, as time goes on and the digs in Jerusalem provide more information, I am sure that will change."

"But it sure seems there is enough information available to indicate they were married," Sarah interjected, as if hoping he could verify their marriage.

"Even if I agreed with you, the fact is, Sarah, it is all circumstantial. There is no definitive proof. Everything we presently have is circumstantial. For example, the Gospels tell us it was Mary Magdalene who went to prepare Jesus's body for burial.

"In those days, Sarah, no woman would touch the naked body of a dead rabbi unless she was family—much less tend to, wipe, and wash the blood and the perspiration from his private parts, unless she was his wife. And it appears that for almost three hundred years, until the Council of Nicaea, the Gnostics and even some of the Christian persuasion believed Jesus and Mary Magdalene were married." The priest clenched his hand in kinetic identification of his beliefs.

At this point, David discussed his digs in Jerusalem and said he was a little disenchanted by the entire situation, as most of the archeologists were not there to find and rebuild old places but instead to find either relics or treasure buried long ago. "Specifically," he said, "the hunt for relics seems to be the new gold. A great number of archaeologists in Jerusalem are looking for bones of Christ. They have made monumental digs at the Church of the Holy Sepulcher, the place where many believe Christ is buried. Personally, I think they are going to be extremely disappointed. I say this not because of Bible lore but because I do not think he was ever buried there. I also believe, as does Father Jacques, Christ is buried here, somewhere in Southern France, with Mary Magdalene."

Sarah was surprised by this statement as she, as most people, believed Christ died on the cross.

"Well, that may be to some people," Dave said, "but I have read the Gospels according to the Gnostics, who happened to be ever present in Jerusalem during the Christ era and for the three hundred years thereafter, just as Father stated a few moments ago, and I have come to the supposition that Mary Magdalene had a plan. As stories go here in Southern France, a ship bobbed and tossed its way at sea and landed here, and on the ship was Mary Magdalene with others, one being an extremely sick and wounded individual. Incidentally, there is an old painting depicting this very incident, picturing a very sickly individual. I now believe that sickly looking individual was the body of Christ!"

After such a detailed dissertation filled with a great number of deductions, assumptions, and inferences, Sarah decided to let her other questions drift to the back of her mind, useable for another day.

The meeting ended on a note of disbelief on Sarah's part and the beginning of a new chapter of beliefs based on those of Father Jacques Cronin and her wonderful new inamorata, David.

The good father was right when he earlier said there was a belief in Europe of a Jesus bloodline, as Sarah had done her homework in this area. But Father Cronin was wrong that his housemaid was not without faults. She had heard every word of the conversation that took place about the replication of Jesus and was anxious to tell the story. As a result, she told someone, who told someone, who told another. Eventually, the rumor made its way to Francois Bigotat of the local Provence newspaper, who embellished the rumor and placed it in the paper as a small third-page piece titled "American Woman Believes Christ Will Be Reincarnated."

12

The next few days were spent with Sarah and oftentimes with David traveling back and forth between Aix-en-Provence and Marseilles, visiting the most prodigious libraries they could find.

"This is fun," David said while passing Sarah's chair, letting his hand slide over the nape of her neck.

"What's fun?" Sarah joked. "Your continual attempt to raise my temperature or the research you're supposedly doing?"

"Naturally, the research. It reminds me of my college days," he replied while attempting to read the Gospel of Mary. "Why would you think anything other than that would be easy?"

"Oh, I don't know. Maybe it's the way you look at me, like a wolf after he has quarried his prey, with his fangs dripping, just waiting for the kill," Sarah mused as she gave a come-hither smile, causing David to drop the Mary Magdalene Gospel.

"Oh, I do, do I? And what makes you think this wolf has his quarry cornered?"

"That's an easy answer," Sarah replied, licking her lips. "Because I'm the prey. I know it, and I love it. Now does that answer your question?" She smiled an award-winning smile. "Now get back to work and read what Mary told the apostles about Christ's teaching."

"I will do that, but—" David began.

"But what?" Sarah said.

"Well, for the last week, we have been involved with the story of Mary Magdalene and have dismissed your conspiracy theory."

"No, that's not exactly true. It's just that I'm stuck and don't know where to go from here. Do I try to question the pope and ask him what's going on? I don't know where to go. It's not like traditional research where you can go to a library or read journal articles or survey some particular segment of a population. I'm just at a dead end."

David was extremely interested in resolving Sarah's dilemma. He thought for a moment and then said, "What about starting a letter campaign to some of the church fathers, the pope included, and see what comes out of the woodwork?"

"That's a good idea. Do you think any would respond, or would they brush it off as some crackpot just looking for attention?" Sarah questioned, her enthusiasm mounting.

"If we phrase the letters correctly, I don't think they could take the chance that information of that nature could be let out to the public. In fact, if the church has anything to do with it, I should think they would do anything to cover their tracks."

Sarah's started thinking there might be light at the end of the tunnel. The remainder of the afternoon was spent going through the writings of first- and second-century writers who attempted to unravel the Christian versus Gnostic story.

The trip from Marseilles back to Aix-en-Provence was uneventful but for the fact that David had to swerve the car to avoid hitting a doe that had wondered onto the highway.

By the time they reached Sarah's hotel, the sun had gone down, and the streetlights were beginning to flicker.

"Want to come up?" Sarah asked in a voice sounding more like a plea than a question.

"Now?" David responded quickly. "How could I refuse an offer like that?"

After parking the car and removing several cases loaded with research findings and other related paraphernalia, the two made their way past the hotel's front desk.

"Bon noir, Mademoiselle and Monsieur," the desk clerk announced.

"Bon noir," David replied. "Do you have a copy of today's *Provence* newspaper?"

"Oui, Monsieur, I do have one in the back room." He left to retrieve it.

"If you don't mind, I think I'll run up to the room while you wait for your newspaper," Sarah said, indicating that a call of nature beckoned.

David laughed at Sarah, as she looked like a little girl afraid she would wet her pants.

About twenty minutes later, David arrived at the room with the news for his lover. "You made the news," he said.

"How so?" Sarah asked, thinking this to be another of David's stories to make her feel better about her family situation.

"It says here that an American is intent on bringing Christ back to life and has the medical background to do it. That she herself was a product of the very procedures that would be used to bring Christ back."

"What?" Sarah responded as she ripped the newspaper from David's hands. "Do you think Father Jacques told this to the news people?" she asked, hoping that was not the case, as she felt a special kind of relationship with the priest.

"No, Sarah, I don't," David responded, half-certain and half-hoping that the priest was not complicit. "Father Jacques would never divulge a confidence like that. He's a priest for Pete's sake. Think how many confessions he has heard over a lifetime. No, no, he wouldn't do something like that," David continued, fervently desirous of exonerating his old friend. "Who else is aware of your story?" David forced a serious look of concern.

"Let's see," she responded, her eyes incapable of leaving the newspaper. "Let's see, there is you," she started, her eyes looking over the top of the *Provence* issue with a questioning look.

"No, Sarah, don't even go there. It wasn't me." David jostled his shirt collar, as if to say, *Look at me. I'm innocent.*

"Don't worry." She laughed, finding a bit of levity apropos at this stage of their relationship.

"That's good," he responded.

"Well," she said, "aside from you and Father Jacques, there is Sister Mary Theresa, my friend at DANNAR, Jayne, and my other friend Victoria."

"That seems like a tight group, with none having anything to gain by telling such a story. I'll go down to the paper tomorrow and see what I can find out. I know the editor. Maybe he can shed some light on where the story came from and who gave it."

"Impossible. I never said that. Where are they getting this information from?" Sarah flinched as she finished reading the article.

"It doesn't say anything about the source. It does identify you as an expert in the reproduction and artificial insemination field." David looked seriously at Sarah, but she could tell by the telltale upturn of his lip that he was enjoying every second of her real family conundrum.

"This is the epitome of yellow journalism," she said as she crumpled the paper and threw it across the room at him. "This is the epitome of yellow journalism," she repeated.

"You are absolutely right, but it may be a blessing in disguise," David, the ever-positive doctor, said.

"I don't know how the news media picked up a story like that without checking any of the facts or concerns with me," Sarah lamented.

"Simple," replied Dave. "This is 2020. The days of factual news reporting went out with people like John Cameron Swayze, Walter Cronkite, and Edward R. Murrow. Today's reporters and newspapers care only about stories. Truth is an anathema to the facts. Lying or outright fabrication is the norm in today's journalism."

13

It was late afternoon when Father Anselmo picked up the telephone and placed a call to Jim Hill at the DANNAR corporation.

"Good morning, Father Anselmo," Hill began in his traditional glib manner. "How are things going over there?"

"Not so good, Mr. Hill," came an officious reply. "First of all, it's not morning here, in Rome—it's late afternoon—and secondly, your presentation the other day spooked the members of our committee."

"How so? I thought I gave you a complete understanding of the procedures used for replicating an individual from DNA and RNA specimens."

"You did, and that is precisely what troubles us," Father Anselmo replied with an obvious element of fear in his voice.

"What is it, Father?" Hill sipped his coffee, awakening to the fact that one of the company's major clients was dangling on the edge of possibly ending their relationship with DANNAR.

"Well, Mr. Hill, the committee is in a quandary over whether to continue doing business with you or just closing up shop and letting our attempts and failures sink into the past."

"Oh, Father, why would you want to do that when we are so close to accomplishing our goal?" Hill responded, as though he was in the confessional booth making an act of contrition.

"Mr. Hill, you said you are a practicing Catholic, so you must understand the gravity for the church in pursuing the venture we—or should I say you—started."

"I do, Father, and I understand that Catholicism as we know it would cease to exist if we acknowledge that Christ was married, had a child, or both. However, just think of the rapture and glory of bringing Christ back for the fulfillment of his ministry. Then, on the other hand ..." Hill racked his mind for the one thing that would keep the Anselmo group in DANNAR's pockets. "Then, on the other hand," he continued, "why does anyone have to know?"

"Know what? Know that we were responsible for such a glorious feat?" came a confused response from the priest.

"No, Father. Why would anyone other than us have to know how the DNA was obtained or from whom?" Hill replied.

"You mean, if I understand what you're saying, you could have the records extinguished, so no trail could be obtained."

"That's correct, Father. They could be so far buried or destroyed they would never again see the light of day." Hill would us any ruse that would keep this large client happy and satisfied.

"Could you do that?" the priest asked, half believing Hill and the other half being very skeptical of his intentions.

"That will not be a problem. In fact, I just wrote a memo to do just that for all our past and future ventures."

"And what happens when other companies in this field understand and incorporate the practices that it must be an offspring that is necessary for replication?" Father Anselmo asked, trying to cover all avenues that could blow up in the face of the church.

"That's not a problem, Father. First, our research teams are so far ahead of the power curve that it will be years before anyone can perfect the program to the extent that we have. By that time, if we find the remains of Christ's children, the issue will be passe. And, Father, no one will care." Hill laid his final move on the table that would hopefully assuage the priest.

"Well, Mr. Hill, you are persuasive, but there is no guarantee that you can keep this hidden indefinitely. And that bothers me. I do believe your last point has merit, and I will present it to them this evening." Father Anselmo, not one for words, abruptly ended the conversation.

"Gentlemen," Father Anselmo addressed the group of priests gathered to make a collective decision about the viability of continuing the replication program.

The meeting lasted for almost two hours, and the final decision lingered, awaiting the decision on two issues. The first was the confidentiality of the DANNAR organization, and the second was that the confidentiality of the program must remain among themselves. Of particular concern was that the pope and other organizations in the Catholic realm remain in the dark until, and if, the replication became a reality. On this second point, all were unanimously in agreement. There was disagreement about the confidentiality issue with the DANNAR corporation, but the bigger picture overrode those concerns.

At eight thirty in the evening, Father Anselmo placed a call to Jim Hill in New York. "OK, Mr. Hill, it's a go. What do we do next?"

The question caught Hill off guard, and the usual confidant response was replaced with one of doubt. "Well, I suppose your team needs to do some research on several issues. The Gnostic Gospels and the information of the first three hundred years have Christ as being married and having children. I think I would start there. You know, there was a recent discovery in Jerusalem of graves marked as Christ, Mary Magdalene, and children, but no one gave the discovery any creditability. Then there is the French belief that Mary Magdalene made her way to Europe in a childbearing way, and, if I remember my time in Provence, the child was named Sarah. So, Father, you may have to give some credibility to the Gnostics if we are going to find a match."

"I think you have a point. It's not something that I care to believe, but as a researcher, I can't afford to dismiss it," the priest reluctantly replied.

"One more thing, Father. Doesn't your Eastern Orthodox community, who reveres Mary Magdalene, also believe she was pregnant when she hightailed it out of Jerusalem? And what about the Quran? Don't the Muslims also have similar beliefs? And—"

"OK, OK," Father Anselmo said with an exhausted exhale. "Enough is enough. You made your point. *Sarah*," he said, stressing the name as if a thorn in his side. "If the pope heard this conversation, I'd probably be excommunicated, stoned, or both."

Father Anselmo's reference to the days of old was comical to Hill, and he responded, "At least you have a good sense of humor, Father."

"That is not a sense of humor, my son; it's close to the fact. We're gambling everything on your ability to do what you said you can do. I sure hope to hell you people know what you're doing."

"Don't worry about that, Father. If you provide the right relics from which we can extract enough DNA, you are going to be a hero and, in all likelihood, the next pope."

"Wouldn't that be nice? I like the ring of it already. Pope Anselmo Brugundini," the priest said.

"I thought you might like that." Hill then repeated the name, implanting it deeper and deeper into Anselmo's psyche.

14

The next afternoon, Sarah returned to the hotel after she and David decided to get cleaned up and head out to one of the local bistros for some fine wine complemented by Camembert, figs, and fresh French bread.

"Mademoiselle Sarah, may I speak with you?" the desk clerk called out as Sarah was about to enter the elevator.

"Yes, of course." She smiled as she walked across the marble floor to the hotel's front desk. "What may I do for you?" she questioned in her finest high school French.

The desk clerk smiled at her broken French and responded to her in his best English. "We have received almost ten telephone calls today from a woman saying she desperately needs to contact you."

"That's interesting," she said. "No one knows I'm here!"

"A Miss Vickie Henderson from Kansa City called and said she desperately must get a hold of you. Each time she called, she gave her telephone number so I would not forget it. It is 1-816-555-1943, and she said to make sure you call as soon as you arrive."

Sarah was ecstatic to receive some communication from a friend back home. The first thing she did as her room door slammed behind her was to have the hotel switchboard place a call to the Kansas City number.

"Hello, Vickie," she said. "It's so good to hear your voice. How are things in KC?"

"Fine," Vickie began before being cut off by a jubilant Sarah.

"I completely forgot to call you and thank you for all the service you provided on TWA and the fine hotel arrangements you made. Everything was excellent," she said, feeling ashamed that she had dissed her newfound friend with such a major faux pas on her part. "I've been so busy over here."

"Well, yes," Vickie replied. "That's obvious."

"I am so sorry. It's totally unlike me to get so involved that I forget to say thanks to someone who has done so much."

"Don't worry about it. I enjoyed doing it. So, on another subject, how are you doing?"

Sarah took over the conversation and for the next ten minutes described her involvement with the nuns, her acquired interest in Mary Magdalene, her new beau, David, and her meeting with Father Jacques.

"What about DANNAR and the replication system they have perfected and the possible replication of Jesus Christ? Is that still in play?" Vickie probed.

"The concern I have over my origins and things like that are of concern, but where does the Jesus thing and the DANNAR corporation enter that picture?" Sarah asked.

"Hmm," Vickie said on the other end of the line. "Do you get American newspapers over there?" the flight attendant questioned.

"I'm sure somewhere in this town there is one. Why?"

"Well, my good friend, you are front-page news over here, and last night, a segment of *Nightline* was about you, your reincarnation story, your search, and DANNAR's complicity with some unknown party to bring Christ back," Vickie said. "According to today's *Kansas City Star*, the story was picked up by Reuters and has spread around the world like wildfire."

"Oh my God." It was all Vickie could discern coming from the Aix-en-Provence end of the line before the line went dead.

Vickie tried unsuccessfully for the next fifteen minutes to reconnect with Sarah, but calls to the room were unanswered. Vickie called the front desk a left a message: "Have two weeks. Vacation coming up. Will fly to Marseilles this evening and be in Aix-en-Provence in the morning. Sounds as though a friend's shoulder could be needed. See you tomorrow."

Sarah's first thought after letting the phone drop in utter despair was to call David. But then, this was not really his problem. Maybe instead she should find out what her friend Jayne thought and see what the DANNAR corporation thought of the article.

"DANNAR. How may I direct you call?" came the sound of someone totally disinterested in the job she was doing.

"Yes," Sarah responded after asking herself if calling Jayne was a good idea.

"Who would you like to speak to?" came an impatient question.

"Oh, yes, I would like to speak with Jayne Anderson," Sarah stated.

"And who may I say is calling?'

"Just say an old friend," Sarah replied, not wanting to divulge any information that would reveal her identity.

"I'm sorry. Company policy says we must have the individual's name before we can place the call," came a typical bureaucratic reply.

Sarah thought for a moment and then said, "Tell her an old high school friend Mary is in town and would like to talk with her."

"I'm sorry, ma'am, but I cannot place the call without knowing your full name."

"OK." Without thinking, she said, "Magdalene."

"All right, Ms. Magdalene, I'm placing your call now to Jayne Anderson. Have a nice day." She ended her involvement without giving a thought to the caller at the other end being Mary Magdalene.

"Well, hello, Ms. Magdalene, and what are you doing today to upset the world?" came Jaynes acknowledgement of Sarah.

"With that as an opening hello, I guess the cat's out of the bag," Sarah replied while attempting to compose herself.

"What the hell did you do, girl? You have this place in total turmoil with the reincarnation story." Jayne laughed. "I haven't seen this much activity around here since Dolly was cloned."

"How bad is it, Jayne?" Sarah timidly asked.

"Well, let's see. On a scale of one to one hundred, I would conservatively estimate it to be ninety-nine point nine. The Catholic Church, our largest client, has a priest on his way from Rome to apparently discuss the viability of continuing the account. The pope just last night completely disavowed the rumor that the church was attempting to replicate Christ, and to top that all off, I think the DANNAR corporation has a hit man looking for you," Jayne said. "Way to go, girl."

"You have to believe me, Jayne. I have no idea where that story came from," Sarah confided in an almost apologetic mood.

"You don't have to apologize to me, sweetheart. I would, however, if I were you, immediately withdraw any money you have in either your IRA, 401(k), or retirement plan before these arrogant bastards think about somehow freezing them. As the old expression goes, Sarah, your name around here is lower than whale crap."

"I'm sorry," Sarah said.

"Listen, Sarah," Jayne began in her motherly fashion, "you have nothing to be sorry about. You were searching for your roots and stumbled on some unlikely information that you must have told someone about, and they blabbed it to the press. It happens all the time. And in addition to all the ethical malpractice you uncovered, you have these male chauvinist pigs running around as if their gonads were tied, like a bull's are before a rodeo bucking contest."

"Would it do any good if I called the president of DANNAR and explained what happened?" Sarah questioned, her naiveté showing.

"I don't think that would be a very smart idea at this time, Sarah. Apparently, there are enough people looking for you now. The press is going to interview your professors from Stanford and Washington University this evening on national television, with some snippets from your childhood supplied by your adopted parents."

"Oh my God!" Sarah exclaimed. "I forgot about them. Jayne, I need to call them right away. I will get back with you. Thanks for your shoulder. It's nice to have someone you can trust." Sarah abruptly ended the call just before Jayne replied.

"Anytime, honey. We haven't had this much excitement around here since Bill Clinton's famous cigar act."

Sarah immediately placed a call to her St. Louis residence and explained the situation to her parents. She then contacted David and filled him in on the happenings of the morning.

15

The next morning, Sarah rented a car and drove early to the Marseilles airport to meet Vickie. While waiting at the passenger pickup zone, she had the opportunity to obtain a copy of yesterday's *Washington Post* and read the article on page 1 about the woman who was going to replicate Jesus Christ.

What is wrong with these newspapers? she thought. *Can't they get anything correct?* The article identified her as being a deranged woman in her early fifties who had a vendetta against the Catholic Church. *That's convenient,* she thought. *Back home, they bend the truth to fit the liberal politicians, while over here they pander to the conservatives. Too bad we can't switch venues and get some more accurate reporting of the news back home.*

Vickie was immediately noticeable in the crowd congregating around the carousel. Her appearance was impeccable. She was the only passenger dressed in clothes that looked as if she owned the airline.

After the enthusiastic reunion of the two, Sarah asked, "What's with the garb?"

"This old piece?" Vickie replied, placing her arms across her chest and making a half curtsy. "This is my travel outfit. When we fly nonrev, the company requires us to look professional, unlike the guy with the John Candy look over there who looks like he just came out of a pigsty and has BO to boot. It's really disgusting the way people dress today."

The drive to Aix-en-Provence was filled with reacquainting themselves with the Mary Magdalene story—the reincarnation hullabaloo, as the press had identified it—and, most importantly, the new man in Sarah's life.

When they entered the hotel, Sarah advised the desk clerk that Ms. Victoria Henderson would be staying in her room, and would he please give her a room key and extend to her every courtesy.

"That will not be a problem, Mademoiselle Sarah, but she must sign the register and a credit voucher for anything charged." Vickie immediately complied, and the two, like children, hustled their way to the elevator.

Before they could open their room door, the telephone rang. It was David.

"Good morning," he cheekily addressed Sarah. "How was your night? Any more contacts from the people abroad?"

"No," Sarah replied, "but Vickie arrived this morning, and she's going to share my room at the hotel for the next few weeks."

"Oh," David responded as if a toy had just been taken away from him.

"Don't worry. I'll make it up to you," Sarah responded, recognizing the underlying reason for David's concern.

'The conversation continued while Vickie, knowing she was the subject of that extended conversation, removed herself to the bedroom, allowing for more privacy with David.

"Look, in view of the fact that the walls apparently have ears, how about if we take Vickie out to the lavender fields where we first went?" David suggested.

"Good idea," Sarah replied. "But," she whispered, "we can't do the things we did."

"No kidding!" David said. "Too bad. I was so looking forward to our next trip out there."

The bantering finally ceased when Sarah said, "I can't wait for you to meet Vickie. She's such a wonderful person. I often think of her as the sister I didn't have."

The remainder of the morning was taken up with the two going over the happenings of last week and the news stories that were circulating about Sarah and her alleged reincarnation scheme.

"Whom did you talk to about the replication issue? Isn't that what you called it?" Vickie questioned.

"The only person that I had a serious conversation with was Father Jacques. But he has told David he had nothing to do with the article, and David believes him."

"Well, somebody had to tell somebody to get this thing in the newspaper. What does the local newspaper editor have to say?" Vickie asked with an incredulous look of disbelief on her face.

"David knows the people at the Aix-en-Provence news, and they said they picked up the story as a rumor making its way among the poorer sect of the town," Sarah replied.

"And they believed it enough to put it in the paper? Whatever happened to good, sustainable reporting? They cannot do that. Don't they need some background in fact?" Vickie ranted. "And why aren't you pissed about it?"

R. W. Kay

"I was when I first heard it, but then I thought back to some of the bullshit our papers back home put out, especially about our president, and I thought if the US papers can put out unsubstantiated trash about him, there is little I can do about it," Sarah responded with a look of acceptance.

"But ..." Vickie hesitated, looking for the precise word to describe the Aix-en-Provence original story. "Yellow journalism. Yellow journalism," she repeated, now more confident that she was on the right.

"You are absolutely 100 percent correct. It is unethical, but it sells newspapers," Sarah replied with a tone of *let's move away from this discussion*. "It's a dead issue, Vickie. There's nothing we can do about it, so we have to move on."

But Vickie was not content with Sarah's argument. She was fierce in her desire to protect her friend from the harassment of stories with little foundation and filled with innuendos.

"Just think," Sarah began in her final attempt to assuage Vickie's predisposition to fight city hall. "How would you like to be the president of the United States and put up with all the fake news he contends with? This is the same thing, only on a smaller scale. It's just unusual that it was picked up on a national scale without more research being done. In short, Vickie, the cat's out of the bag, and you can't fight city hall." Sarah smiled. "So, let's move on."

"OK," Vickie responded with a look of disbelief. "Where do we go from here?"

"That's a good question. I'm not sure. I'm not sure what to do next. I'm torn between proceeding further with chasing down my mother's background and researching my newfound interest in Mary Magdalene, who seems to have been the victim of a massive apostolic plot to discriminate against women."

"That was, what, over two thousand years ago? What do you propose to do about it?" Vickie situated herself on the couch, assuming the lotus position.

"I really don't know except I think and feel the lady got screwed by a bunch of misogynist apostles, the Catholic Church, and history in general. I think, from what I have read to this point, that the church needs to restore her and women in general to their rightful position," Sarah replied, now sounding like a member of the women's movement from her college days.

"That's a hell of an undertaking." Vickie listened intently as Sarah rambled on.

"And if the church is behind this plot to use virgin nuns to carry through pregnancy an experimental baby, for whatever reason, it's an indication of their lack of concern for women in general. So, you see, Vickie, the two quests are interrelated."

"What did you mean about restoring Mary Magdalene to her rightful place?"

"The world is changing, Vickie. We can now do things medically that other generations would view as pipe dreams. As you now know, we can replicate people from two thousand years ago and beyond, given the ability to extract DNA from their relics. That is how far medicine has advanced. In the field of archaeology, I was told by David they are finding documents and other paraphernalia that is shedding a much different light on many things we have taken for granted. And, of course, Mary Magdalene happens to be one of them."

"Like what?" Vickie said, showing a legitimate interest.

For the next twenty-five minutes, Sarah explained her dissertation about Mary Magdalene, her involvement with Christ, and the rebuke she took at the hands of the apostle Peter.

"So, you see, Vickie, had the leadership of the apostles, namely Peter, been less antifemale, the first pope may well have been Mary Magdalene rather than Peter. Just think how different things would be if Peter and his friends weren't misogynist from the get-go."

The telephone rang, interrupting the train of thought. It was David. He was calling Sarah's room from the telephone at the front desk rather than knocking on Sarah's door. He thought this gave more of an impression of propriety.

"Good morning, sunshine. Are you ready for your trip to the lavender fields?"

"Yes, we are. We will be down in five minutes," Sarah responded.

"Fine, me lady," David replied. "Your chariot awaits."

16

A week later, David was keeping Vickie entertained while Sarah was recuperating from a minor bout of the Asian flu. As with Sarah, Vickie was interested in seeing the sights of Provence and exploring the tapestries surrounding the patron saint of Southern France.

Unlike her friend Sarah, Vickie was more to the point in her meeting with Father Jacques.

"I was told by Sarah that you admonished her to keep quiet about her conspiracy theory and—"

Father Jacques Cronin interrupted, saying, "That is correct. As I told her, there are some who may not take kindly to someone, namely an American, announcing the possibility of replicating Jesus Christ. Many people in this area of the world look at the Americans as becoming more and more Godless, and for someone to say they can revive the Savior is blasphemy. And who knows what could arise from that!"

"And yet, shortly after telling you about her conspiracy belief, it winds up in the local newspaper. That does not sound coincidental, Father. It sounds purposeful. Who did you tell about my friend's concerns?" Vickie kept applying pressure to see if the priest would provide some information.

"I told no one," the priest, now on the defensive, replied, "but ..."

"But what, Father? My friend Sarah is sitting in her hotel room and shivering at the thought that some anti-American religious zealot is going to attack her—or worse. So, what are you thinking, Father?"

"Do you remember, David, the breaking of the glass during our discussion?"

"I sure do, Father, and you dismissed it as nonessential because it was only the housekeeper."

"That's right, and you're right David. Mrs. Pauget could have overheard our discussion, but even if she did, there is no reason for her to go to the news media," the priest, ever protective of his housekeeper, stated.

"Well, could you call her in here? And let's find out," Vickie pressed.

"But even if it was Mrs. Pauget, what value is there in confronting the poor old lady?" Father Jacques defensively responded, now recognizing that the leak rested at his feet.

"Because, Father," Vickie said, "there is a young lady, my friend, who has been put in extreme jeopardy when all she wanted was a little advice on Mary Magdalene. And now she is sitting in a strange hotel room afraid that the boogeyman is out there, waiting for her. And it would be nice to know how this mess got started."

"OK, Ms. Vickie, you made your point. I will summon Mrs. Pauget."

The old woman appeared twenty minutes later in her somewhat tattered housekeeper garb.

"Yes, Father, what can I do for you?" the old women questioned upon her arrival.

"These folks have some questions to ask you about the other day when David here"—he gestured toward David, who was standing at the window, looking out at the rectory flower garden—"was with a young lady, and while we were talking, you broke a glass in the next room. Do you remember that day?"

"Yes, sir, I do," the old woman replied. "I cleaned the mess up while you entertained them."

"That's right, Mrs. Pauget. I thought you might remember that day."

Although the good priest was trying to downplay the magnitude of the situation, Vickie wasted no time in questioning Mrs. Pauget.

It was immediately apparent that the old woman was in fear of losing her housekeeping job, but after twenty minutes of reassurance provided by Father, she finally opened up about her part in conveying the information to her good friend Mrs. McGinty, who herself, according to Mrs. Pauget, was a bit of a gossiper.

Vickie turned to the priest and, without any indication of respect, closed the meeting by saying, "I guess we now know where the leak is and how the press got a hold of the story."

Meanwhile, back at the hotel, Sarah had just received a notice from the desk clerk that a letter had arrived for her.

"How would anyone know how to reach me here at the hotel?" she thought out loud.

Jon, the desk clerk, overhearing her conversation with herself, answered. "That is easy to understand, madam. The *La Provence* of Marseilles published an article three days ago about the Christ, how you say, regeneration ... replicating ..."

"Replication story?" Sarah helped him while being curious as to what he was going to say.

"Yes, madam, that is it the replication of Christ story." He stopped, looking at her seriously. "Do you really think you can do that?" he asked, expecting her to answer in the affirmative.

"I don't think so," Sarah responded. "It's just a news trick to try to sell more papers."

"In that case, madam, it must be working because it is hard to find a paper anywhere."

"So, what did the article have to say the other day that would provide someone with my address and location?"

"Nothing much about you, except about the replication story again and a great plug for the hotel, identifying us as the hotel of your choice in Aix-en-Provence."

"Oh my God!" Sarah said and then made her way to the elevator and back to the sanctuary of her hotel room.

The afternoon in Provence was gray, and so was Sarah's desire to open the envelope sitting on the desk in her room. There was no return address label on the envelope, and since no one knew her whereabouts, whoever sent it was obviously outside her scope of known friends. Her first thought was to call David, but as before, she thought this was her problem, and David should not be bothered with such trivialities. With wide-eyed expectation, she picked up the envelope and looked for any possible indication of the origin. The postmark indicated Marseille, but she knew no one in Marseilles. And since the envelope had no discernible advertising, it was not typical junk mail. With great trepidation and justifiable fear, she grabbed the hotel letter opener provided in the desk and held the envelope up to a light to possibly see the contents. But the envelope itself was made of heavy bond paper, not permitting light to reveal its contents.

Oh well, she thought. *Here goes.* She slid the letter opener under the flap. Then suddenly she stopped and froze, thinking, *What if this is a letter bomb from some of those people that Father Jacques warned me about?*

Regaining her composure and already having the letter opener halfway through the envelope, she continued. When completely open, the envelope revealed a one-page standard-sized white sheet with a typed note she could see before completely unfolding the paper. It said:

> Yahweh will send upon you the curse, the panic,
> and the threat {in everything that you undertake},
> {until you are destroyed and until you perish quickly}
> {because of} the evil of your deeds in that you have
> Forsaken me. (Nehemiah 28:20)

Now it was time to call David!

Both David and Vickie arrived at the hotel at approximately four thirty in the afternoon. Vicky had just returned from an afternoon shopping trip, and David had returned to his shop after the joint meeting with Father Jacques. Vickie was the first to enter the room.

"Guess what?" she excitedly blurted out. "We found the culprit in the suspicious telltale yellow journalism scheme."

Sarah, however, showed little interest in hearing who the culprit was, nor at this point did she care.

"What's wrong?" asked David. "We thought you would be elated over our news. He looked at Vickie with curiosity.

Walking around the room as a person whose jitters forced them to seek relief, Sara handed the note to David. Her shaking hands gave away the gravity of its contents.

Both David and Vickie read the letter. Vickie was the first to console Sarah.

"Oh, honey, let's get on a plane and get out of here, back to Kansas City, or even to your family's place in St. Louis where you know people love you."

"Just a minute," David interjected. "People love her here in Provence," he said, looking at her with eyes indicating just who loved her.

"I don't think that's necessary. First of all, this was obviously written by someone who doesn't know what he or she is talking about, and generally people who indulge in this type of threat don't ever carry it through."

"What makes you think this is someone just making casual threats?" Vickie asked.

"Well, two things," David began. "First, the quotation is taken from the Old Testament and has no relevancy to New Testament aspects such as the resurrection. And secondly, the citation is all wrong. It is not a quotation from Nehemiah; it is from Deuteronomy, which to me indicates the writer is either unaware of where it comes from or forgot and just put in whoever would suit his fancy. In either case, it sounds like a pure amateur to me."

"What about the church or the DANNAR corporation?" Vickie asked while Sarah listened intently. "Maybe the mistake is deliberate to make us feel it's some amateur."

"I don't think so," David answered while pulling his chin as if in deep thought. "Neither of those two organizations would try to scare you if their real intent was to kill you; they would just do it."

17

AT 4:55 p.m. Provence time, 10:55 a.m. New York time, Sarah's phone rang. It was a call from the DANNAR corporation, namely Jayne Goodwin.

"Hello, honey. How are things going over there?" Jayne said.

"Not so good. I think someone over here is seriously out to kill me," Sarah said while fighting the tears welling in her eyes.

"I wish I was there with you to help with the insanity of what's going on."

Sarah dried her eyes. "I can tell you're brimming with some tidbit of information."

"Oh, indeed I am, Sarah. Indeed I am," Jayne said. "That news article has created a major stir around here. I almost didn't get this information, as the powers that be are either burying or shredding anything and everything related to a master file called simply Revival."

"So, what's the connection?" Sarah asked, trying to focus the information on her specific concern.

"It seems that both you and your cousin in Kansas City, plus a myriad of others, are all mistakes."

"What?" Sarah recoiled. "What does that mean?"

"Are you sitting down?" Jayne asked.

"As a matter of fact, I am. Why?"

"Because honestly, what I have to say is going to floor you," Jayne said, her stark warning about what was to come.

"I'm sitting down, Jayne, and I think I'm prepared for anything you're going to throw my way, so fire on. I'm ready and willing to stand," she said, mimicking her adopted father's onslaught speech used whenever he was confronted with unpleasant information.

Jayne took a breath and responded, "Apparently thirty or so years ago, when DANNAR researchers stumbled upon the belief that people could be replicated, they sold their idea to someone in the Catholic Church. In a short period of time, the parties agreed to try the possibilities out, with the intention of replicating Jesus."

"What? Are you serious?" Sarah said, processing the information at a much slower pace than Ms. Goodwin was delivering it.

"Yes, I am, Sarah, and here comes the kicker. Both you and your cousin were the results of that experiment."

"No shit!" Sarah's said. "And I guess at that time, since they didn't have the right combination of male genome from a sibling strained to produce only the male elements, any chance of success was impossible?" Sarah surmised.

"That would appear to be correct!" Jayne said. "I don't know much about your biological parents, but if they did find the remains of Jesus Christ, as we discussed before, you could be related to the Holy Ghost, the Virgin Mary, Joseph, or some rascals living a little over two thousand years ago. Somehow, they knew that you particularly did not make the grade. In your case, it was probably because you were a female. Isn't that amazing? Two thousand years later, we are still agonizing over the same church tactics. I'm not sure how they figured out your cousin was not the Savior. I guess we'll never know that one."

Sarah was mesmerized by the story but bounced back and opined, "So that's why they chose nuns to carry the fetus, because they wanted to create a birthing environment that closely mimicked that of the Christ story, and virgin nuns fit that bill."

"I think that's true," Jayne said. "But now they've found the real formula for replication. And if Christ was mortal and did in fact sire an offspring, and DANNAR and company can find them, we are going to shortly experience the rapture of the second coming. What do you think about that?"

"Not a great deal at this point. I'm more concerned about the person sending me threat letters. So, who is the person corresponding with DANNAR that is intent on doing this idiotic program?"

"I'm not sure. There's something scratched on one of the file flaps. It says ANSELMO. That could be a contact, a location, or who knows what."

"You're right. It isn't much to go on, but it's a far cry better than what we had up to this point. I'll see what I can do with it and let you know later. Thanks for all your help, Jayne. I do really appreciate your help with this."

After getting off the phone, Sarah thought back to the opening of the conversation and telling Jayne about the death threat. It seemed to fall on deft ears as Jayne brushed it aside and went on to something else.

Why would she do that? Sarah thought. *Why would she dismiss the statement out of pocket? Why?*

18

Several days later while Sarah was still recuperating from her bout with the stomach flu, David was met outside his office by a man identifying himself as a UNESCO representative. The gentleman named Herr Hans Weber asked if he could speak to David about some pressing issues in the field of archaeology.

"Why of course," David casually replied. "Anything for a UNESCO representative."

David understood individuals of such stature never contacted archaeologists in person unless a possible assignment was being considered.

"Won't you come into my shop of antiquities?" David said, stumbling over the right words to say to this prodigious figure.

After making some small talk and observing the vast collection of relics from David's numerous digs in Jerusalem, the man wasted no time in coming to the reason for his visit.

"Dr. Behlke, are you aware of the political unrest that has taken place in Sudan recently?" Hans Weber asked, attempting to ascertain David's archeological world understanding.

"Well, sir, I can't say that I'm an expert on the politics of Sudan, but I am aware of the fact the Sudanese people recently overthrew an authoritarian rule, part of which was inspired by a movement of national identity," David replied, hoping his answer would satisfy this stranger.

"That is precisely correct. There is a movement of national pride taking place in Khartoum, and their history and discovery of their ancient roots has become the rallying cry of the governments decenters. For that reason," he continued, as if reciting a rehearsed speech, "the Sudan minister of antiquities has asked us to peruse a short list he has prepared, looking for someone to ramrod a program to uncover 'the glories of Sudan's past,'" he said, raising his hands and making the symbolic quotation gesture.

"Based upon my limited exposure of the promise of Sudan and the country's relationship with Egypt, I should think that digs could reveal the information they require," David replied, feeling a bit uneasy about his lack of knowledge of the history in the Sudan environment.

"Don't feel distressed by your lack of Sudanese history or a working knowledge of the possibilities abundant there, Dr. Behlke. That is precisely what the minister is looking for, someone without any preconceived ideas."

"So," David said, now taking charge of the conversation, "where is this conversation leading? I presume from your statements a position may be in play here. Is that correct?"

"Not just a position," the small-statured man resembling Toulouse-Lautrec continued, "but the handling of the total operation of finding a new past for the Sudanese people."

The conversation continued for several hours and was only cut short by the constant and intermittent buzzing of the telephone.

"Excuse me, Herr Weber, but I think someone wants to talk with me in the worst way. I apologize for the interruption, but I better answer that call."

"Of course," Herr Weber replied. "I think you are right; someone does require your attention. Go on, answer the phone. This discussion can wait," Weber graciously answered.

David searched for the telephone receiver that was buried under a group of relics from his Jerusalem digs and answered in a professional manner loud enough for his visitor to hear.

"Good morning. Dr. Behlke, Provence Archaeological Office," he announced as the guest smiled at the professionalism of the refined doctor's greeting.

"What's with the formality?" Sarah questioned, thinking she had maybe misdialed.

"It's just practice," he announced, directing the conversation so that his guest would not get the wrong impression of his professionalism.

"What may I do for you today?" he continued.

"I don't know what's going on over there," Sarah said, believing David's replies to be totally out of character, "but I just received the morning mail, and there are five notices that I deserve to burn in hell for my blasphemy, while two others are pure and simple death threats," Sarah announced, her voice now quivering in fear.

"Oh, Sarah, I'm so sorry!" Dave responded, feeling a deep sense of concern for the feelings of the first and only love of his life. "Stay there. I'll be over shortly. I have a friend who is the head detective of the Aix-en-Provence re municipal, and I'm sure he can help with this problem. So just stay there. I will be over ASAP." Dave hung up the phone.

"Problems?" the small-statured man questioned as he began to rise from his chair while placing a dossier on Dr. Behlke's cluttered desk.

"No, not really," David replied, forcing a smile to offset any feeling of despair or concern over Sarah's predicament.

"Good. I'm glad to hear that. It sounded a bit awkward. I trust all is well," Weber said.

"Yes, sir, Herr Weber, all is well. Thank you for your concern," David responded. "Everything is in good form!"

"Marvelous. That's the way everything should be," the UNESCO representative responded as he departed David's shop.

As soon as his guest had turned the corner of Cours Mirabeau and rue Ste. Christian, David picked up the telephone and placed a call directly to the prefect of the Aix-en-Provence Gendarmes. The phone was answered immediately on the other end.

"Aix-en-Provence Gendarmes. May I direct your call?" said the no-nonsense officer.

"Yes," David answered resolutely. "May I please be connected with the prefect?"

"And who may I say is calling? And what is the nature of the call?"

"Tell him Doctor David Behlke is calling, and the subject matter is personal," David said in his most professional and patronizing tone.

"Yes, sir, I'm connecting you now," the officer replied, as if knowing the parties had a personal knowledge of each other.

"Dave, how have you been, you old son of a gun?" said the prefect.

"Just fine," David began. "Well, maybe not totally fine."

"What's wrong, old man? You haven't lost your golf swing or anything like that, have you?" Granger Bisset replied, thinking this was maybe a ruse to get him on the golf course where David's prowess was always difficult to overcome.

Granger and David had been friends ever since they first met on a golf course ten years before. David's skill and ease of delivery provided him the perfect requirements to teach and improve Granger's game, an improvement for which Granger always seemed grateful.

After the playful bantering among golf partners, David explained the situation in which Sarah found herself and the concern he had over the death threats she was receiving.

At the end of what seemed to be a lengthy conversation, Granger indicated he would send his best man, Alain Boucher, chief detective, over to the hotel to meet with both David and Sarah. He did admonish David to be careful, as the religious zealots were very unpredictable even though the threats might be nothing more than threats.

David called Sarah to tell her about the meeting with the inspector and what she should expect.

At eleven thirty on the dot, Alain Boucher entered the hotel. His stature and steel-blue eyes made him the epitome of what one would expect an inspector to look like.

David, waiting in the foyer, greeted him and accompanied him to the room, where he met Sarah and her friend. Not being one to expect surprises, Detective Boucher was moved by the presence of Vickie. Shortly after being introduced to Ms. Henderson, he came right to the point.

"I am to understand Mademoiselle Sarah has received several death threats because of the statement that appeared in the local newspaper over a week ago. Is that correct?" he questioned Sarah.

The interview and the interrogation lasted for almost two hours, with the final summation being that this type of threat, albeit unusual, almost never eventuated into one where action was taken. "However, just in case we are dealing with some deviant personality, I'm going to station a plainclothes detective outside the building. Just in case," he repeated.

The thought of having a detective within calling distance seemed to satisfy both Sarah and David. He did, however, imply that Sarah should be quarantined to the room until the situation could be totally reviewed and checked out.

"And how long do you think that will be?" Sarah questioned, obviously annoyed by her restriction.

"I'd say no longer than about three days, as all these letters are postmarked locally, and we should have little trouble running these crackpots down."

"And what is his name?" Sarah asked as Detective Boucher was about to depart.

"Whose name?" Boucher responded as he was leaving the hotel room.

"Oh yes, I did forget that didn't I? His name is François Bisset, and no, he is not related to the prefect." After that statement, Alain Boucher withdrew with the death threat letters in hand.

19

The meeting the following morning at 605 Third Avenue on the forty-second floor of the Burroughs Building was anything but friendly. The DANNAR people were blaming members of the church for creating the situation with Ms. Sarah Birch by failing to keep the information concerning replication quiet. The members present from Rome cited the fact that Ms. Birch was a representative of the DANNAR corporation who found it advantageous to bring the story to the press.

Contently listening to the barbs being thrown back and forth, Jack Newman, the CEO and DANNAR chairman of the board, raised his hand as if to say enough was enough.

"Have you ever thought that maybe neither of our competing factions is to blame? Maybe this woman's stumbling onto this story was just an act of fate that each of us failed to recognize the potential for. Even if she has 100 percent of the story under her belt, which I doubt she does, how has it hurt us? We are on the verge of producing the greatest event known to man, the hastening of the second coming of the Savior." He immediately received the attention of everyone present.

"Suppose we found the ingredients to the equation we know will work, what is the worst thing that could happen? First, Father Anselmo, I don't think there would be any doubt that you would be elevated to the next pope. The loyal members and even those disloyal members of the church would flock back to the congregation just to be associated with the rapture of the event. And, Father," he said, addressing the priest as if no one else was present, "just think what could happen even if we, or you, could not find the missing ingredient. You would have every Catholic and Christian alike trying to find it for you.

"On the other hand, there is a win-win possibility for DANNAR too. Can you imagine the number of people who, believing in the Christ possibility, would want their long-lost relatives revived? I don't see a downside. Do you?"

"But, Jack" Father Anselmo said, standing, "what if the pope found out about it before the ingredient to the equation, as you call it, was found? What then?"

"Father, do you believe the pope or anybody else would dare to confront the tide that would be generated when the actual particulars are revealed and the consequences of those particulars are understood? Could the church withstand such demand? I think not." Newman sat back in his chair, letting the discussion rest on the ears of those present.

"Suppose we do nothing, as you suggest," Father Gallucci, a longtime member of Father Anselmo's inner guard, said. "What do we do about the girl?"

"Nothing," replied Newman. "She has already started the fire and apparently is out of ammunition to finish her fight. So, we just let her hang out there to dry, looking like the foolish little urchin she is. She cannot hurt us anymore. Her fifteen minutes of fame have passed."

The meeting ended a few hours later, with all in attendance agreeing with the Newman position, although Anselmo wanted more time to renegotiate the cost of doing business with the DANNAR corporation. The request fell on deaf ears, as the possibility of success was within range according to the CEO.

20

Two days after Sarah's quarantine, or house arrest, by the Aix-en-Provence constabulary, David received a phone call from Vickie asking for his help in getting to Marseilles, where she had to pick up her passes for the return flight to Kansas City a week hence.

"But of course. I'll be glad to drive you down to the airport," David responded. "But first I need to talk with Sarah and ensure everything is all right with her and that she's being treated well by the local authorities."

"Not a problem, Vickie replied. "In fact, here she comes now, fresh from the shower.

After a brief lover's introduction, David told Sarah of Vickie's need for transportation to the Marseilles airport. Sarah congenially agreed that David should help Vickie any way he could and that she would be in her hotel room waiting for their return, and possibly the three of them could dine in the hotel dining room that evening.

"Sounds like a plan," David said. "Tell Vickie I'll be over in about forty-five minutes."

At ten fifteen, David arrived at the hotel and found Vickie waiting in the lobby.

"Why are you down here waiting? I thought I would come up to the room and get you," David said, seeing Vickie looking a little distressed.

"Did you see that goon that just walked out of the hotel as you were walking in?" she asked.

"No, I can't say I did. Why?"

95

"Well, Sarah and I got a little concerned when we saw him looking up toward our room from across the street. He was standing in the pharmacy entrance just staring. We both became a little nervous, and I decided to come down and see if I could get a better look at him and call the detective if necessary."

"And then you ran into him in the lobby?" David asked.

"Yes, I thought I saw him at the front desk, and when I went over to get a closer look, he just shot by me, almost knocking me down in his haste to get out of the building. That's when he bumped into you." Vickie's words showed the nervousness she was feeling.

David convinced Vickie to take a seat and let the initial concern dissipate while he confronted the front desk clerk about the unknown man's intentions.

"I don't know who he was," the clerk replied to David's questions, "but he did ask the room number of Mademoiselle Birch and her telephone number."

"And did you provide either one?" David anxiously questioned the young clerk.

"No, no, no," the young man repeated. "That is against the hotel policy, so I did not give him that information."

After several more questions, David and Vickie returned to Sarah's room, where David called Granger Bisset and provided him with the information.

"Sit tight. Stay there. Alan and I will be over shortly," the prefect announced.

After two hours of discussion and interrogation of hotel personnel, Granger Bisset told David he thought Sarah was safe in the hotel and he should continue with his trip to Marseilles, as Detective Boucher and Constance Clermont would be stationed in the room and seated outside Sarah's door.

The drive to Marseilles was uneventful but for the conversation about the morning activities and the strange man who almost knocked Vickie down.

Arriving at the airport, Vickie exited the car and made her way to the ticket counter, where she exchanged her voucher for a class 9-1 employee pass to the United States. The time involved was noticeably short, and was long for David waiting in the car, it only took about fifteen minutes to complete.

"Pretty quick, huh?" Vickie teased David. "Now, as a way of thanking Sarah's knight in white armor, how about letting me treat you to a French afternoon lunch by the sea?"

"Oh, I don't know. Don't you think we should get back, given this morning's happening?"

"I don't think it's necessary. I told Sarah I was going to ask you to lunch in Marseilles, and she thought it was a good idea.

"She did, did she?" David smiled, his white teeth glistening against the brown backdrop of his tanned face. "OK, if she said lunch was OK, so be it. Lunch it shall be."

The two searched the Marseilles Mediterranean coastline for a place that was away from the conventional crowd and still had a menu worth reading.

They found such a place called the Vin de Set Restaurant, whose wine selection and coq au vin luncheon, along with the blue skies and blue waters, made the experience memorable.

"This place is marvelous," Vickie commented.

"It sure is beautiful here, isn't it?" David academically asked, not expecting an answer.

"Yes, it is," Vickie responded. "I'm not sure I want to go home. Maybe I'll stay here for the rest of my life."

"There is no doubt this is the living, but the ever-present question is, can you afford it? Or better yet, can your American lifestyle slow down to that of Southern France?" David questioned as he looked out to the vast Mediterranean Sea.

"I know, but I think I would like to try it!" Vickie responded as she sipped her cabernet sauvignon. "Maybe I could get transferred to the TWA international flight attendant program and be stationed at Orly or Charles de Gaulle."

"Is that a possibility?" David asked.

"Probably a pipe dream, but, you know, without dreams, there isn't much of a future, is there?"

"No, Vickie, I think you have a point there. Without a dream, there is not much, is there?" Dave responded, thinking about Sarah's dream to find her roots, only to wind up fighting the world.

"What is your dream, David?" Vickie asked, twisting the cork from the wine bottle in a most playful way.

David was oblivious to the adventurous advance being made and responded that he found Sarah most interesting and would love if she would consider possibly marrying him and traveling with him on his numerous digs.

"I think she would like that," Vickie replied, wishing in her heart that she had been the one to find David, or at least someone like him.

David, beginning to feel a tinge of emotion in Vickie's responses, excused himself for a few minutes and made his way to the restroom, where he thought out a way to respond to Vickie outside of the flirtatious venue that was beginning to creep into their conversation.

Coming down the path to the luncheon location, David noticed that Vickie was resting her head on the table, as though she had found a perfect spot for her respite.

"Vickie, are you all right?" David asked, approaching the table. At that point, he noticed her head was resting in the coq au vin. He reached for her head and tugged it to realize her face had been blown off by the force of a bullet striking the rear of her head.

"Oh my God, oh my God!" Almost paralyzed by the tragedy, he was helpless in doing anything but sitting down and crying over Vickie's lifeless body.

As the Vin de Set personnel began showing up to observe the incident, Dave asked one to call the local police and report a murder had taken place. At the same time, he used his cell phone to dial the Aix-en-Provence prefect of police, Granger Bisset, to advise him of the situation and to elicit his help with the local Marseilles Gendarmes. Granger acknowledged David's request and said he would be in Marseilles within the next couple of hours.

Now David's biggest trial awaited him, calling Sarah and giving her the news that Vickie was dead. As he waited for the Marseilles police to arrive, he kept thinking about what he was going to say to Sarah. Her death was not a coincidence, especially as the morning had been spent talking about the man Vickie identified in the hotel lobby who acted strangely.

It did not take long for the local police to arrive on the scene. They were followed by an ambulance and a coroner. Ten minutes after arrival, the coroner pronounced Vickie dead and had her body placed in a body bag, put in the ambulance, and sent to the morgue for further evaluation.

The police wasted no time in surveilling the premises, taking pictures, and asking everyone in the vicinity of the table questions as to what they had seen and heard.

Then it was David's turn. His interrogation was more advanced than the others, as he was the deceased's escort of the day.

"Mr. Behlke—oh excuse me. Dr. Behlke," the chief Marseilles detective addressed David after seeing the name on his American passport. "Where were you at the time of the shooting? What was your purpose in Marseilles? And do you have any acquaintances in Marseille?"

"I'm well aware of police tactics, Detective Monfre," David told the police officer. "The three-question tactic, to see which I answer first, is as old as the Mediterranean Sea here. I am not complicit in this murder, if that is what you are trying to find out, so ask the questions you want answers to, and I will gladly comply," David responded with the shrewdness of an individual who had been questioned by the best in his worldly discussions with customs officers, border patrol officers, and numerous pseudo law enforcement officials that archeologists encountered in their assignments.

"Fair enough, Dr. Behlke. Your directness and knowledge of criminal procedures and investigations is refreshing." With that, Detective Filipe Monfre spent the next two hours asking questions and receiving answers from Dr. David Behlke.

Just about that time, Prefect Granger Bisset arrived, introduced himself to Detective Monfre, and apprised him of the Aix-en-Provence stakeout of Dr. Behlke's fiancée and the morning's occurrence with the surly man at the hotel.

"I should hope we can work together on this unfortunate murder, and if you have any rationale for holding Dr. Behlke, he can be released to my recognizance."

"I don't think that's any problem, Prefect," Monfre began. "It seems he is an innocent bystander, just as is everyone else at this establishment."

"That's an interesting assessment, Detective Monfre. What brings you to that conclusion?" Bisset questioned.

"The bullet," Monfre said.

"What about the bullet?" Bisset asked.

"From the position of the deceased's head on the table, the massive destruction of the front of her head, her face was completely obliterated," Monfre said. "We can assume the culprit fired a high-powered military-type rifle from over a half mile or even more away. With Mademoiselle Vickie sitting in this location and this vantage point, she was an easy target for anyone in the hills along the shoreline. Just between you and me, Prefect, Dr. Behlke's convenient stroll to the restroom and the placement of Mademoiselle Vickie in her position could be looked at in more detail for possible complicity. I have no proof of that, but it is a possibility, just for your edification and future reference."

"Thank you for that, Detective Monfre. I shall keep that in mind," Bisset replied as he mulled over the possibility.

When David and Granger were alone, Granger asked if David had called Sarah and explained the situation to her. When David replied he had yet to do that unpleasant bit of business, Granger suggested he wait until they returned to Aix-en-Provence so they could approach Sarah together.

21

The mood was a bit somber as David and Prefect Granger Bisset entered Sarah's hotel room. Although the two attending police officers did not apprise Sarah of Vickie's death, they were aware of the happenings that morning. Sarah, although having no information, was, because of perceived attitude differences in police personality traits, aware that something was going on.

"Good morning," Granger said to the two officers. "Where is Miss Sarah?"

With a nod of her head, Officer Claremont indicated the bedroom.

Both David and Granger took steps toward the bedroom, but David raised his hand, indicating he would take the news to Sarah.

As he entered the bedroom, Sarah immediately asked, "What's wrong?"

"Well," David said, "we had a bit of a problem in Marseilles this afternoon."

"What was it? It's Vickie, isn't it? What happened? Where is she?" came a rapid-fire succession of questions from an astute Sarah.

"She's dead, isn't she?" Sarah continued, her eyes welling with tears.

David was astounded by Sarah's intuitiveness.

"How did you know?" David was somewhat relieved he had not been forced to be the bearer of bad tidings.

"I just had that feeling. Something inside kept gnawing at me all day—that I should never have allowed her to go to Marseilles, much less let her wear the Gucci blouse she gave me when we were in Kansas City. What exactly happened?"

David then recounted the events of their time in Marseilles, the luncheon, and then the event, deleting the specificity of how he found her body.

"Oh my God!" she exclaimed. "Oh my God! I set her up! I set her up! It was my life somebody wanted, not Vickie's, not Vickie."

Sarah spent the remainder of the day in bed, alternating her sleep pattern with bouts of vomiting over her best friend's demise.

Meanwhile, the police and David canvassed the hotel personnel to ascertain if anything had been left out of the earlier attempt to determine the identity of the rude and surly character Vickie had encountered in the morning. Nothing, however, had changed. The identity of the individual was a complete mystery.

"I did talk with the Marseilles police, and based on the angle of the bullet piercing her head, the terrain of the area, and the foliage and tree cover, the only place where a clear shot could have been taken was over three-quarters of a mile away from a ridge on a nearby hillside. That would seem to indicate the shooter followed you to the location and then had to find a location, set up, and fire. Also, at that distance, the individual would have to be an expert marksman. Adding this all up," Granger continued, "the possibility of this all happening in the time frame you identified seems almost impossible."

"I agree," David replied.

"How did you decide on this particular restaurant and where you were going to sit? And how long were you gone from the table?" Granger asked his old friend.

"To the best of my recollection, Vickie ultimately decided on the restaurant after we had driven around the area for about forty-five minutes, and she selected the table. I suppose I was away for about ten minutes."

"That may be the best ten minutes of your life," Granger surmised. "If you had been across from her, with the force of the bullet, you would also be in the morgue right now," Granger posited, to see the facial reaction of one now becoming a potential suspect in Vickie's demise.

"Granger, that last question seems to imply that the possibility might exist that I had something to do with Vickie's murder," David said.

"No, no, not from me, but I'm posing questions they will want the answers to!" Granger replied, closely observing David's body language.

"I hope, Granger, you don't think I had anything to do with this," David protested.

"Don't jump to conclusions just because I asked a couple of questions," Granger replied, now studying Doctor Behlke's denial more closely than before.

22

Sarah remained in her self-administered quarantine for three days after the death of Vickie. Much of the time she spent in agony, crying over the events of the past few days. David tried contacting her several times during this hiatus to suggest that she take up quarters at his villa estate located a short distance outside of Aix-en-Provence. But when he finally did contact her, she listened to his proposal but flatly rejected it on the grounds of propriety. David, however, would not take no for an answer and ultimately convinced her that paying for a hotel would in due course deplete her cash reserves, and why do that in view of the potential long battle looming to find the mysterious Anselmo fellow's whereabouts.

"You're right, you know," Sarah replied to David's overture. "I am going through my capital reserves rather quickly."

"I know you are. That's obvious," David responded on the other end of the somewhat antiquated, by US standards, telephone line.

"But, David, how would that look, especially if the press got a hold of it? They would have a field day."

"Screw the press," said David. "This is Europe, by the way, not the tawdry US. Our minds are not constantly in the gutter. So, there is no impropriety here, and besides, I love you, and I want to protect you."

Sarah, quick to pick up on the love overture, replied, "You love me, David? Is that what you said?"

"Yes, it is Sarah. I've been wanting to say that since our first rendezvous, the day we met. I never had such a feeling of sheer emotional and mental joy until being with you. I mean, really being with you. I now know this feeling is the real thing, and I hope there is some mutuality on your part." He paused, waiting for a reply.

"Me too!" Sarah coyly replied. "I love you, David. Oh, how I love you."

The feeling of exhilaration was wonderful for both parties, and the small talk between them took up much of the afternoon.

"So, Sarah, does this mean you will accept the invitation to stay at my abode?" David pressed.

"Of course it does, you big lug," Sara responded, giving David his new love-inspired nickname.

"Big lug, big lug, where did that bit of definition of me come from?" David playfully asked.

"You figure it out, Doctor. You're a smart guy. I'll give you a hint. I became acquainted with the expression that first day in the lavender fields," she said, laughing.

"Oh. Oh that." David flushed shades of red on the other end of the line. "I can see I have fallen in love with a nasty little girl. No, a nasty little bad girl. And you know what? I love it. So, I will gladly be your big lug if you will come and stay with me … for the rest of your life." David grimaced and tightened his jaw muscles, wondering if he had gone too far. After all, it did sound like a proposal of a long-term relationship or possibly marriage.

Taken back by the question, Sarah hesitated with her reply and then asked very seriously, "Are you asking what I think you're asking?"

David, now faced with a monumental decision, was confronted by Sarah's question of put up or shut up. Having never been in this position before, he quickly weighed the alternative of never meeting someone as interesting as Sarah, someone as intelligent, someone as attractive.

"Yes, Sarah, I'm thinking the same thing you're thinking, and although this feeling has never occurred before, this now becomes a formal proposal. This is not the way I envisioned a proposal would be, especially over a telephone; however, Miss Sarah Birch, would you do the honor of being my wife?"

"Yes, yes, I would, and I would love to be your wife!" Sarah stuttered in her enthusiasm. "But, David, I'm concerned that our lifestyles may be too great to be overcome. That is a major concern to me," Sarah frankly sputtered.

"What does that mean, Sarah?" David needed to understand the mind of this ravishing doctor of medicine and doctor of philosophy.

"It means you have your life pretty well defined by who you are and the position you have been conditioned to hold; your education and vocation created that path. Me, on the other hand, I have probably destroyed my life's vocation by virtue of what we are now seeing as a prelude to disaster, something that a virtuous person like yourself would not, or should not, involve themselves in. In short, David, I'm not sure you and I fit together. I'm not sure," Sarah persisted, "I'm not sure, in retrospect, that I'm the right person for you. And I say that with only love for you."

"You can't possibly mean that, Sarah. We fit well together, and if it's the archeology and time away from one another, I don't have to be involved with exotic digs or globetrotting to other parts of the world. I can just as easily find employment back in the good old USA with a land developer or some other construction-type operation. My occupation does not have to be paramount. That could and possibly should be reserved for your medical and/or teaching career. All in all, I think we would make a surprisingly good pair, no matter what avenue we jointly pursue. So, Sarah, don't worry so much. When the time comes, we'll be able to make a joint decision that will work out the best for both of us."

"I hope you're right, David. I guess, no matter what we would like, we are what fate wills us to be. And I presume she will be the indicator of whatever will be, so I reserve my right to continue worrying about our situation and will think about it tomorrow."

"OK, Sarah, you do that! And while you do, I'll just keep preparing for our walk down the aisle," David responded with an air of total confidence.

23

"Enough is enough," Sarah told David as she reminisced over her dead friend Vickie's life and the fact that she had been the recipient of two attempts on her life and numerous letters identifying her as a prospective target for several crackpots.

"What do you want to do?" David asked, having compassion for Sarah's concerns but not believing she should go off the deep end in her endeavors.

"I want to confront this priest Anselmo's and tell him what I know and how easy it will be to bring the house down on him and his little band of ruffians, including my former employer, the DANNER corporation," she replied.

"Are you serious? Do you want to confront the man face-to-face? If he is the individual responsible for these death threats and possibly Vickie's death, and you confront him personally, what makes you think you'll get out of Italy alive?"

"I don't know, but I want to confront the man face-to-face. After all, he's responsible for my screwed-up childhood, my cousin's screwed-up childhood, and who knows how many others' in his attempt to reincarnate Christ. From what little I know of Christ, I believe even he would be against such a preposterous scheme. So, David, I've made up my mind to go to the Vatican, or wherever I can find this roach, confront him, and find out why he caused me to have a life with no parents. Are you with me, David? Will you go with me to Rome?"

"Sarah, if you don't know the answer to that question by now, you'll never know it. Of course I'll go to Rome with you. I just hope you're doing the right thing." David hung up the phone, debating whether to call his friend Granger Bisset or just leave well enough alone.

After mulling over the alternative for several hours, he concluded that he must back Sarah fully if he hoped to get her to the altar.

Three days later, they were on their way to the Italian peninsula, through France and Italy, stopping along the way in Nice, Genoa, and Florence, arriving at the Eternal City at three o'clock on Thursday afternoon.

Sarah had never been to Rome and was overcome by the beauty and splendor that accompanied every corner of the Eternal City.

David, on the other hand, who had been there many times before, was exhilarated just showing Sarah around the city.

"Our first stop will be the Hotel Memphis, an old pension that has been remodeled into a fine and classic hotel. I lodged at the Memphis over twenty-five years ago when the proprietor was an old woman who made toast with juice for breakfast," he reminisced.

"Is it near any attractions?" Sarah asked.

"Attractions? The Hotel Memphis is in the heart of Rome, a five-minute walk from the famous Trevi Fountain and the Spanish Steps. It's hard to find a better location," David gushed.

"What else is interesting about Rome, the hotel, and whatever, since you sound as though you are the public relations guru for the place?" Sarah laughed.

"Well," David began, "since you put it that way, the Memphis is set in a restored fourteenth-century building on a quiet side street in central Rome. It's just a short hop from Rome's main shopping street, Via Del Corso, and a five-minute walk from Barberini Plaza. In short, Sarah, it's a gem in hiding from the average traveler. Now, aren't you glad you're with me?"

"Aye, aye, Sir David." Sarah saluted. "I'm glad I made your acquaintance."

The following day and weekend were a veritable festival of seeing the sights and shopping at the stores and hotels along the Via Vittorio Veneto, one of the most famous, elegant, and expensive streets of Rome.

"See how lucky you are to have me," David said to Sarah at their Sunday-evening dinner at the hotel.

"I'm very lucky, you sweet man, but I feel so ashamed that I had such a wonderful time with you while Vickie lies dead in a casket in Aix-en-Provence," Sarah said as a tear trickled down her cheek.

24

The following Monday, Sarah, holding hands with David, entered the palatial offices of the Holy See, looking for the location of Father Anselmo.

"And in what division of the church does Father Anselmo reside?" the extremely officious receptionist asked.

"I don't know," Sarah replied, sounding as though she was small and insignificant relative to the grandeur of the surrounding edifice and the accouterments of history maintained on the walls and ceilings of the building.

"I think he may have something to do with medical research or just medicine in general," Sarah continued.

"I'll check our roster of priests and see if I can find a Father Anselmo in the medical field, but in the meantime, would you please sign the register and indicate who it is you wish to see and the time of your check-in?"

While the young woman searched the Vatican files of priests involved with medicine, Sarah complied with her request, signing, without thinking, her name and the reason for her visit, which she indicated to be "to pass on information from an old friend."

After about twenty minutes of waiting, the receptionist turned the register toward herself, searched for the name of the party seeking a Father Anselmo, and pressed her speaker call button. "Ms. Birch, Miss Sarah Birch, please report to the receptionist desk."

"Yes, Sarah Birch, that's me," she announced, approaching the receptionist's desk.

"Yes, Ms. Birch," the receptionist answered, "I cannot find a priest named Anselmo in our medical documents, nor anyone with that name in the facility of Rome, but I did find three priests with that name in our total collection. Would you be interested in their locations?"

Feeling a bit dejected with no priest within the medical area, Sarah reluctantly said yes.

"We have a Father Patrick Anselmo, who is the pastor at the Church of Our Lady of the Snows in Belleville, Illinois; another in Perth, Australia, at the Church of the Holy Trinity, whose name is Father Enrique Anselmo; and a third, a Father Patrick Anselmo, who is doing missionary work in Africa. He is in the town of Sotoubona, Toga, at the Church of the Notre Dame de Togo."

"And that's it, only three?" Sarah responded, showing signs of being annoyed over the indication that none of those had the possibility of having any direct relationship with the pope.

"I'm sorry, madam. That's all I have for a priest with the last name of Anselmo," the receptionist said as she turned her attention to another visitor.

Discouraged, Sarah and David left and headed to a local café that faced the Trevi Fountain.

"So, there were only three Anselmos in the entire Catholic Church priesthood," David stated as the couple sipped their glasses of Chianti and waited for lunch to arrive.

"I'm afraid so," Sarah replied. "Now what do I do?"

"Are you positive that's the priest's name? Where and how did you obtain his name?"

"You know, that's a good question," Sarah replied. "I don't know. I think after what happened with Vickie, I'm beginning to lose my mind."

"I don't think that's the case. You're as sharp as ever, and you will ultimately remember this guy's name. Maybe you should call your friend at DANNAR and see if you have the right name." David replied as he began eating his hefty Italian salad.

"I'm a bit reluctant to do that after what has transpired. Plus, I'm becoming paranoid over with whom I share information and with whom I don't," Sarah confessed.

"What brought that on?" David asked with a look of surprise. "I thought you had a buddy there who gave you good information."

"I did at one time, but something she said has caused me to question her loyalty."

"Are you sure Anselmo is this priest's last name?" David asked, without genuinely thinking about the possibilities the question raised.

"Good point, David," Sarah said. "No, I'm not sure, and you're right—his last name could be something else. You are so brilliant, David. Thank you."

David looked up from his salad, a piece of tomato hanging from his lip, and asked, "About what?"

"About Anselmo's last name. You are correct. It's probably something else. Tomorrow we will have to go back to the Vatican and have the snobby receptionist search for every priest with a middle or first name of Anselmo. Then maybe we can find this snake." Sarah was giddy over the possibility of potentially finding the individual responsible for her ruined childhood and quite possibly the death of her friend Vickie.

Morning came, and Sarah and David prepared for their sojourn back to the snobby Vatican receptionist. But before leaving the hotel, they beat a path to the dining room for a continental breakfast of coffee, juice, and a chocolate croissant. While sitting there, David found on the next table a copy of yesterday's *New York Herald* newspaper and began reading the sports page, searching for the scores of his favorite team, the Kansas City Royals.

"How are they doing?" Sarah asked, her mood very playful since she believed answers to her questions about her ancestry were just around the corner.

"Not so good, honey," David replied while glancing over the top on the paper.

"And how about my Cardinals? Where do they stand?"

"A little better than the Royals," he responded, pressing his lips together as if to imply not simply better but *much* better.

"How much better?" Sarah pressed, knowing the rivalry that existed between two Missouri cities.

"Well, the St. Louis Cardinals are in first place, two games ahead of the Chicago Cubs." David swallowed his pride. "I sure hope the Roman cardinals will be as productive for you if we ever get that far with these insane workings of Father Anselmo or whatever his name turns out to be."

"Me too," Sarah said while buttering her croissant. "Me too!"

25

The remainder of the morning was spent preparing for meeting with the Vatican receptionist and how Sarah and David would approach her.

Meanwhile in Genoa, at the Church of the Immaculate Conception, Father Anselmo was on the telephone with his Dominican counterpart in Marseilles.

"Good morning, Father Junipero. How is the search going for Sarah?" Anselmo immediately asked.

"Which Sarah?" Father Junipero Serra replied, not indicating any concern for the question posed. "Do you mean the Sarah residing somewhere in Aix-en-Provence or the other one?"

"You know damn well what I'm calling about." Anselmo grimaced while puffing on a cigarette, trying to keep his emotions intact over the frivolous responses from the Dominican priest.

"Oh, that one, the one that allegedly graced our shores some two thousand years ago. No, we have not found her yet. Do you think she might be hiding in Aix-en-Provence also?" He laughed.

"No, you moron," Anselmo said. "You may think this request is a joke, but I assure you, Father Junipero, this no joking matter. So, where has your assignment led you?"

"Well, if you put it that way," Father Junipero said, chuckling to himself, "we have sent a staff of seventeen predates out to libraries, churches, graveyards, and city and county recorders of deaths, deeds, and whatever stone we can find to overturn to find your Sarah. If she's here, we will find her. Do you seriously believe that Mary Magdalene had Christ's child?"

"Whether I believe it or not is of no moment to you, Father Junipero. What counts is you finding her," Father Anselmo replied with an air of superiority.

"Will do, Father!"

"Just one last question," Junipero said.

"And what would that be?" Anselmo indicated signs of impatience with the Dominican priest. "Well, what is the question?" Anselmo waited.

"About the girl in Marseilles and the Sarah in Aix-en-Provence, the shooting, and the threats of death." He hesitated. "The church had no part in that, did we?"

"Father Junipero Sera, I assure you, you can rest your simple mind on that subject." Anselmo replaced the receiver on the telephone in his office.

When the line went dead, Father Junipero did the same.

It was now nine thirty in the morning Rome time, and the parties began their trip to the Vatican to find the hidden priest, Anselmo.

"Good morning" Sarah said to the receptionist. "I was here yesterday trying to find a priest named Anselmo."

"Yes, I recall, and I gave you the names and locations," snapped the receptionist in her officious manner.

"Yes, you did, and you were very helpful," Sarah replied, attempting to keep the conversation congenial. "But I think the name I gave you was more likely his first name and not his last or family name, however that works."

"So, I suppose you want me to check for anyone with a first name that matches your request of yesterday. Do you realize how large an undertaking that will be?"

"I understand that. I assure you if it weren't particularly important for me to find this priest, I wouldn't be asking for your help," Sarah said in her best motivational manner.

"OK. Sign the register and fill out the purpose of your visit with the first name of the individual you're trying to locate."

Sarah complied with the receptionist's instructions and accidentally asked a question that would again set her off.

"How long will that take?"

"Do you realize how many people are in the rolls of the Catholic Church? Your request could take anywhere from one to three days, depending on how much time I have to devote to it."

"And shall I call you, or would you contact me?" Sarah asked.

"You can call. The name and number are on the card," she replied while observing the next individual's name on the register. She called out, "Next!"

David and Sarah spent the remainder of the day taking in as many sights of Rome as possible. The Vatican and St. Peter's Basilica were such that an entire week would not allow one to even make a dent in the history and appeal there. Sarah was so impressed with the *Pieta*, located inside the basilica, that she and David observed its beauty for hours.

"Did you know, Sarah, that Michelangelo created another *Pieta* where the Mary holding Christ's body is Mary Magdalene?" David asked, knowing her concern over her insignificant woman, as she liked to call Mary Magdalene.

"No, I didn't know that. Is that statue also here?" Sarah anxiously replied, eager to see Michelangelo's rendition of Mary Magdalene.

"No, it's not. It's at the Duomo in Florence. Maybe, if you would like, on our way back to Aix-en-Provence, we could stop off in Florence and see it," David said, knowing the trip and the sights of Florence would please his future bride.

"David, you are so good to me. How can I ever repay you?" Sarah winked.

"That's easy. You can start by setting a date for our marriage," David responded. His next dig could jeopardize something he thought would never become a reality, her acceptance of his marriage proposal.

"We have a lot to talk about in that regard," Sarah said.

"Like what?" David said, not wanting to sound overly concerned.

"Like a lot of things. I have a profession, and I'm very happy with my credentials and would like to work somewhere where they are needed. Sitting at home in some villa in France alone, waiting for a telephone call from my husband, who is a million miles away digging up some old ruin, is not my idea of a marriage."

"I have been giving that very subject a great deal of attention lately," David replied. "As you know, I don't know where my next dig will be, although I do know I am presently being considered for a very important site that one could invest a lifetime working at. For that reason, I thought we could work together as a team on the dig, or, using your credentials, you could easily work for Doctors without Borders, spending your life in service to your fellow man while I try to find the history of our fellow man's ancestors. I hope it is not a pipe dream, Sarah. I know you and I would make a wonderful team, and your background would be much more beneficial than mine." David continued with his introduction to Africa, hoping he could convince Sarah to at least think about its possibility.

Sarah listened intently to the potential of David's possible Africa assignment that the representative of UNESCO had laid out to him only a few days previously.

"Wow, you have been thinking a lot about our future, haven't you?" Sarah acknowledged. "I can't say this is the kind of marriage I had expected, but it does pose some special considerations that must be addressed. I love you, David, and I want to marry you and be with you, but I don't know if I want to spend my life in some godforsaken east African jungle while you are looking for antiquities. I must admit it sounds interesting, but I am going to need some time to think about this," Sarah sincerely replied.

"I understand," David acknowledged. *I think I understand*, he thought, with a quizzical look.

26

Two days had passed since requesting information on Father Anselmo, during which Sarah and David took advantage of the time to tour the city.

On Tuesday afternoon as they sat in their favorite restaurant fronting the Trevi Fountain, Sarah noticed a man ostensibly reading a newspaper but literally watching them—or more particularly her. Sarah's interest was piqued when he moved toward them.

"David," she said, "there's a man coming toward us, and he has been watching us all the while we've been sitting here—and now he's coming toward us."

David immediately rose from his chair after grabbing the knife that adorned his plate, hiding it behind his back as if to protect Sarah from whatever potential danger might be coming their way.

"Good morning, Dr. Behlke and Dr. Birch. Allow me to introduce myself. I am Inspector Antonio Costa of the Italian Carabinieri, working presently in Rome under the local *capo della policia*, or as you say in the US, the chief of police. Excuse me for my interruption of your lunch; however, I am here on official government business," he said as he extended his hand to David while making a bow in the direction of Sarah.

While shaking hands with David, Inspector Costa produced proof of his identity by showing his shield identification.

"Thank you, Inspector. What can we do for the Carabinieri?" David said.

"Well, sir and madam" he began as he eyed Sarah with interest, "we have been made aware of a threat against the life of Dr. Birch and that the attempt carried out in Marseilles apparently failed only due to misinformation and identification on the assassin's part. We also know you are here in Rome searching for a priest named Anselmo. I have been assigned your case, as we have received information that another attempt on your life, Dr. Birch, will be made again while you are in Rome!" the inspector said.

Sarah looked to David, showing signs of distress and uneasiness.

"How do you know this information, Inspector? Who told you this? We have been having a fine time in your fair city, and no one has bothered us," Sarah said while closely observing the clientele seated in the restaurant.

"We have a system of viable sources, and when we hear news of something like this, we immediately look into it, and if it is legitimized, we take every precaution. For that reason, you have been under surveillance since you registered at the Hotel Memphis."

A series of questions followed, most of which were elementary and designed with the target in mind. But one question kept entering the conversation. "Who is doing this?"

"Unfortunately, we have no idea. Your statement reported in the Aix-en-Provence newspaper about a replication of Christ, I believe that was the way you phrased it, has raised several feathers here in some of the more conservative religions. People here take their belief structures very seriously, and rather than approach anything new or attempt to understand anything new, they immediately cry blasphemy and want to crucify the perpetrator without even listening to the argument. Sort of like the Middle Ages when a person was burned at the stake for witchcraft for explaining that lightning was a common occurrence and not a symbol from God. You, with your educational background, should be aware of this disturbing inability to think," Inspector Costa continued as if presenting his case before the capo della polizia. "And no, madam," he said, turning to Sarah with a look of abject sadness. "At this point, we have no clue who is behind this, but you never know, when you keep turning over rocks, what kind of worms will turn up."

"Am I to understand you condone my trying to find this Father Anselmo fellow and find out his influence with the possibility of replicating Christ?" Sarah was curious to know.

"Madam, I am a devout Catholic, but in my profession, I have learned there are bad people in every religion, and should you turn one up, I would not be surprised. That would not change my belief unless it was the pope himself ordering it." Costa laughed, as if making a statement outside the realm of possibility. "Besides, your research is doing much of the legwork I would be required to do! So, thank you, Doctor."

The conversation lasted for about forty minutes, after which Inspector Costa suggested moving the meeting to a place where Sarah would be less likely to be a target.

The parties agreed, and although the local police station was suggested by Inspector Costa, it was vetoed in favor of the party's room at the Hotel Memphis.

For precautionary reasons, Sarah and David returned to the Hotel Memphis upon leaving the Trevi Fountain restaurant, while Inspector Costa made a detour, returning to the station to see if any more information regarding a potential assassination had come to light.

Upon arriving at the hotel, the pair was greeted by two plainclothes police officers introducing themselves as Officers Bommarito and Lato, the latter being a female assigned as a personal bodyguard to Sarah. An hour later, the inspector arrived at the Memphis.

"Good afternoon," Detective Costa announced to the officers standing outside the entrance to Sarah's room. "Any problems so far?"

"No, sir, everything seems to be in order," Officer Lato replied.

"We checked the room for explosives and the window for potentials where a shooter could find a target. None seemed to exist, but in view of the dossier's indication that the killing shot of her friend was made from over a half mile away, we advised Miss Sarah and her male friend to stay away from the windows and the balcony as a precaution," Bommarito followed.

"Very good." Costa smiled. "Let's go in and see what we can learn about this immediate situation. I think, Officer Lato, you may have your hands full trying to keep up with Miss Birch. My earlier conversation indicates she is highly active and likes to do things her own way. So, stay strong with her, and do your best to keep her out of harm's way."

"I'll do my best, sir," said Officer Lato.

"And, Marcello," Detective Costa said to the other officer, "your job is to keep your eyes open for a possible shooter or any place where one could be stationed. I know that's a monumental job, but I think you're up to the task. That's why I personally picked the two of you for this assignment. I knew you were the people I could count on. It's our job to keep this woman alive. The last thing we want is to have the woman who knows how to bring Christ back to life murdered on our turf. *Capire!*"

"Capire!" came the reply from the two.

Prepared for each of their assignments and responsibilities, they knocked and then entered the room.

27

At four thirty Wednesday afternoon, a call was sent from the front desk of the hotel to Miss Birch's room. As the phone buzzed, Officer Bommarito motioned to Officer Lato to answer the call. "Just in case it could be someone other than a friend."

"Pronto," Lato answered in her appealing voice. "Oh, yes, she is here. One moment please." She held the receiver out to Sarah. "It's for you, ma'am." She smiled. "It's the receptionist from the Vatican."

"Hello, this is Dr. Birch," she answered. "Oh yes, thank you. We will be over first thing tomorrow morning to pick them up. Thank you so much for your help," she repeated as she replaced the receiver.

"There's forty-seven of them," she said, looking at David.

"Forty-seven?" David responded. "That could take quite a while to run down. Are any of them in Rome?"

"No, that was one thing she emphasized. There is no priest with the name of Anselmo in Rome, which comes as a surprise to me."

The next morning, the couple, accompanied by the officers from the *policia de stato*, made their way back to the Vatican office.

"Excuse me," Officer Bommarito said as David and Sarah left the hotel, "is this the way you traveled to the Vatican the other day?"

"Yes, it is," Sarah replied. "It takes us past some of the grandiose sights of your city."

"Well, ma'am, I think we might want to go a different way today. Just precautionary. You understand."

"Oh yes, of course, I understand! I should have thought of that myself, Officer. Good point," Sarah responded, not taking the threat very seriously.

The four took about forty-five minutes to reach the Vatican office, where the receptionist immediately recognized Sarah.

"Good morning, ma'am. Here is the information you requested," she said, handing Sarah a manilla envelope.

"Thank you for your help," Sarah began, "but may I ask—"

The receptionist cut her off and called out, "Next!"

Sarah and David followed closely behind Officers Bommarito and Lato as they left the receptionist's desk and headed for the nearest available library table.

"Excuse me, Miss Birch, but may I recommend a place a little less in the open?" Officer Lato suggested while observing potential locations where someone might hide.

"Oh, sure," Sarah graciously replied. "Do you have a place you would recommend?"

For the next half hour, the parties searched through the names supplied by the Vatican receptionist, and out of a total of thirty-eight names, they immediately dismissed thirty-two due to their location and standing in church hierarchy. Of the remaining six names, one, a priest named Gallucci Anselmo Brugundini, stood out because of his closeness to Rome. He was in Genoa, at the Church of the Immaculate Conception, conveniently located on Sarah's and David's return to Aix-en-Provence.

The next day, contrary to the advice of the *cabinari*, David and Sarah set out to meet Father Gallucci Anselmo Brugundini. The weather was perfect for the five-and-a-half-hour drive partially along the Mediterranean Sea coast.

Father Anselmo's receptionist was older than one would have thought for someone whose boss's title carried the name Guardian of the Truth, the moniker written alongside his office door. Despite this obvious discrepancy, she was very congenial.

"Father Brugundini," she said to the priest, "this is Miss—"

"Miss Sarah Birch," he said, interrupting her. "No need to introduce her. I am well acquainted with Miss Birch, although she doesn't know it yet. Come in. I've been expecting you." He smiled, extending his hand.

His warmth and friendliness took Sarah by surprise, as she expected a hardened individual who relished in having cast so many children aside in the inevitable quest to replicate Jesus.

Walking aside Father Brugundini into the plain but modernly furnished halls, Sarah was taken aback and disarmed by his familiarity with her.

"How is it you say you know so much about me Father Brugundini, or should I say Anselmo?" she said.

"Your choice. Whatever suits your fancy," he replied, again disarming her with his familiarity. "That's simple!" He laughed. "You have been a part of our family for the past twenty-eight years."

"I have? And how is that?" Sarah responded with a look of mysticism and cynicism.

"Sarah, we both know why you are here, so let's cut to the chase. You have been on our radar since your birth twenty-eight years ago. Your background with both medicine and research at Stanford and your brief stint at the DANNAR corporation should have fully made you aware of what transpired."

"I am, but that doesn't make me any more receptive to what has gone on," she responded, with a look of pure disdain for the priest's attitude.

"Let me state it like this, Sarah. You were part of an attempt to replicate our Savior, and as such, you hold a special place in the annals of Christianity. You are the vessel of royal blood.

"Quite some time ago, the DANNAR corporation postulated an idea of bringing Jesus back to the world through the newly known practice of gene splicing. In doing so, it was believed that if—and I repeat, if—we could find viable DNA or RNA from Christ, the process would replicate the Savior."

"But it didn't, did it? Instead, you got me and, I suppose, my second cousin, George Hartman, whose mother is a Dominican nun down in Aix-en-Provence," Sarah responded.

"That is true, Sarah. In fact, all you have said is true," Father Anselmo replied without a bit of consolation in his voice.

"Your mother," he continued, "was a beautiful individual, and as you well know, she died because of complications associated with childbirth. She was committed to the program and for one month after your delivery nursed you for, as she said, the glory of God's beauty."

"What the hell does that bit of trivia mean?" Sarah asked with a tone of unquestioned disbelief.

"I think she felt very committed to what she was doing and wanted to hold this holy child as long as she could."

"But I'm not the holy one," Sarah replied.

"No, you are not Christ, but again, as I said, you are the vessel of holy blood," Father Anselmo replied.

"So, after my mother died, what happened?" Sarah kept pressing for more information.

"Naturally, it became necessary for us to find a decent place for you to grow up; ultimately, we chose Saint Louis, where our order is well ensconced." Anselmo continued without one iota of remorse, which Sarah had expected.

For the next half hour, the priest talked about Sarah's Catholic upbring, her adoption by the Birch family, and her ultimate deviation from Catholic education by her desire to attend a public high school. He talked about Sarah's independence in terms of curve balls that she kept throwing, first high school, then Washington University, and ultimately Stanford. He stated that keeping up with her required so many different avenues.

"Like what?" Sarah asked.

"Like trying to keep up with you so we could provide the money required for scholarships, grants, and other various funds."

"Are you saying that my education was funded by the church?" Sarah let out a gasp.

"Yes, Sarah, that is precisely what I mean. In fact, you were slated to attend a prestigious all-girls Catholic high school in Clayton, Missouri, but you opted out for attendance at a public school in St. Louis. After that, we had you set to attend Notre Dame for your undergraduate work, Georgetown University for your graduate work, and then a stint at Harvard and Johns Hopkins for your postdoctoral education. But, alas, you fooled us on all of them, instead going to Washington University and Stanford. We had to scurry around to keep up with you, but with the help of Catholic Charities, we succeeded."

"I am amazed!" Sarah stood up and walked toward the window, looking out at a statue of a naked David looking back at her.

"And the hardest part was yet to come. That was placing you in a position where your future was to be guaranteed."

"I guess I outsmarted you on that one also, eh?" She turned from the window and returned to her seat, looking at Anselmo with a smile.

"Au contraire, my dear. You did precisely what we had hoped you would do."

"What? Go to work for DANNAR corporation?"

"Precisely. We worked on you for a couple years to get you into that corporation, and we had plans for you their too. But, again, you threw us another curve, and here you are in my office, searching for your roots."

"Just out of curiosity, what was the position at DANNAR that I was being groomed to ultimately assume?" she shyly asked.

"A few years down the road, we anticipated that you would assume the position of chief executive officer. Your educational background and your commonsense approach to most problems made you a logical candidate."

"And, just out of curiosity, how could you pull that off?"

"You know that old expression of never bet against the United States?" Father Gallucci Anselmo Brugundini rhetorically asked. "Well, the same can be said about the church," he empirically stated.

"How so?" Sarah was anxious to hear the particulars.

"Well, in the vernacular, we own 72 percent of DANNAR's common stock, although we have it spread over many accounts so that no one is the wiser. In addition, we carry almost 60 percent of their debt structure. Thus, we are the owners of the company, lock, stock, and barrel, as you Americans like to say. So, see, we own the game, and we could easily fulfill our wishes."

Sarah again left her chair, returning to the window, weighing the next question on her lips. Turning and facing Anselmo, she said, "Then why the desire for me to be dead? The death threats, the letters, the news articles, and, of course, my good friend Vickie's assassination, only because she happened to be wearing my clothes?"

"Sarah, don't be absurd. Why would we even consider such a foolish act? You are our prized possession, and we want the best for you. That should not even be within the scope of your thought process. I can understand how some may feel that way, but surely you can't possibly believe it to be someone within the church," the priest said in his best fatherly manner.

"Then who?" She broke down with tears flooding her face, more for her friend Vickie than for herself.

"I wish I could answer that one, Sarah, but as of yet, we have not been able to determine a specific individual or group behind the threats."

"What do you mean by *we*? Who is we?" Sarah pressed.

"Since this all began, the Holy Alliance, or moreover our own CIA, has been keeping a very close an eye on you while, at the same time, turning over every rock where these types like to hide."

Sarah, unaware of the church's secret investigative arm, then questioned the results of their work.

"First, as with you, we looked within ourselves to eliminate that possibility. Catholics," he resumed, "don't seem to be as ill-informed as the Protestant group, as many Catholics in upper Spain and lower France believe in the Gnostic structure and could go so far as to believe that Christ did not die on the cross. But the Protestants are not quite that broad and from all indications seem to want your scalp for blasphemy. Thus, we have been closely watching a group out of Germany who have sworn that your statements border on blasphemy. Other groups that could also have a losing stake in the outcome, should Christ be replicated, are the Jews and the Muslims. A second coming could very possibly destroy their entire belief structure. Our good friends in the East, the Hindus, Shintos, Buddhists, and others, could probably care less."

"So, you don't know either?" Sarah summarized.

"No, unfortunately, we don't, but we do have some ideas." The priest pulled no punches with his unequivocal statement.

The conversation between the two lasted another half an hour before David entered the office, asking the secretary how much longer Sarah's meeting would last.

"It seems your archeologist friend, David Behlke, is becoming a little concerned about you." Father Anselmo looked at Sarah with the eyes of a concerned parent. "May I make a suggestion?"

"Of course, Father," Sarah said.

"Sarah," he said, now reaching out to hold her hand, "this thing could get a lot worse before it gets better, and with that in mind, I'd like to make a suggestion."

"That's fair," she replied, not having any indication of the framework of the suggestion.

"Good. In our concern for your safety, we have uncovered some things only a very few know. First, we are aware that you and Dr. Behlke have discussed the subject of matrimony and that you are seriously considering his proposal. Second, and something that you may not know, Dr. Behlke has, or will be, offered the position of his life in the pyramid fields of Sudan. That brings my next argument to the fold, and you may say this is none of my business. And should that be the case, I shall never utter it again."

"Are you serious? David is going to get the job of his dreams in the Sudan?" Sarah said. "That's wonderful! Does he know?"

"Not yet, but the offer is on its way," the priest continued. "And that is what I would like to speak with you about."

"I guess after all you have confided in me today, one more piece of information can't be too devastating." Sarah smiled.

"May I then suggest you take Dr. Behlke up on his offer, move to the Sudan, raise children, and in the meantime accept a position that Doctors without Borders is soon to ask you to fill. This will remove you from the field as a potential candidate of assassination, provide a good and happy living, and allow you to pursue your medical and research dreams. No one in their right mind wants to travel to the deepest interior of the Sudan to fulfill some, or any, contract."

Sarah left the office of Father Gallucci Anselmo Brugundini, the Guardian of the Truth, with a new spirit of enthusiasm and optimism but still with a fear that somewhere, someone was waiting to terminate her life.

28

The return trip to Aix-en-Provence was anything but uneventful as the entire discussion with Father Anselmo was rehashed by Sarah almost to the point of ad nauseam. But David's interest kept Sarah enlightening her lover with tidbits that he was unaware of in his dealings with church officials.

"That is all extremely interesting, but what did he have to say about the threats on your life? Does the church have anything to do with that?"

"I can't say for sure that I know the answer to that question, David, but based on the information given to me by the priest, I don't think the church had anything to do with it. In fact, he gave me some insight into who both he and the Holy Alliance believe the perpetrators might be."

"The who? The Holy Alliance? Who are they?"

"Apparently, the church has their own Central Intelligence Agency, and it's this Holy Alliance group. They have reduced their search to a group of malcontents in Germany who consider it blasphemy. And according to Father Anselmo, the Guardian of the Truth, my head could be their target."

"Did you say Guardian of the Truth? What does that mean?"

"Beats me!" Sarah replied. "I only know that based on my conversation with him, I am more inclined to believe him, especially since he is the Guardian of the Truth." She giggled and punched David on the thigh.

"Thanks for that," he said. "You mean in all the time you were in Father Anselmo's, I mean Brigantine's, or whatever his name is, that's all the information you received?" David asked, expecting to hear a great deal more than what Sarah was releasing.

"Well, he did talk for a long time about the replication process, which we already knew about, and he did apprise me of how the church monitored my life throughout my education, my job, my meeting you and—"

"Your meeting me? What does he know about us?"

At this point, Sarah feigned being very tired and wanting to sleep for a while on the return trip. Her ruse was an attempt to keep the information to herself about David's future job offer, the priest's suggestion of accepting David's marriage proposal and then moving to the Sudan, where a pending job offer for her with Doctors without Borders would become a reality. All of this was being weighed in her mind against the knowledge that she could ultimately be the CEO of one of the largest medical research organization in the United States. This dilemma was monumental for the orphan girl who, according to the Guardian of the Truth, carried royal blood.

"OK, Sarah, catch your forty winks, but when you awake, I deserve to hear more about what you were told. OK?" David said as the afternoon sky began turning purple and the lights of the Italian/French countryside were beginning to flicker.

"That's a deal," Sarah responded. She laid her head on David's shoulder, then immediately dozed off.

For the next four hours, Sarah slept while David maneuvered several treacherous mountain curves, arriving in Aix-en-Provence late in the evening. Rather than go to the office and check the mail, the pair opted to head straight to David's living quarters, where they kissed good night and fell asleep.

Early the next morning while Sarah was still slumbering, David decided to drive into Aix-en-Provence to retrieve his mail and to ensure that his office was still intact. As he approached the front door, he noticed what looked like a notice of eviction posted. Getting closer, he could read the typed opening sentence that said, "Martin Luther posted forty-four reasons to leave the Catholic religion. We need only one to want to destroy it, and the name is the Guardian of the Truth, with death to his illegitimate protégée, your mistress, Sarah Birch. Her time is coming, and we know where you live." The missive went on to elaborate on other aspects, but David wasted no time in returning to the car and making his way home.

"David, David," Sarah cried when she heard the car pull into the driveway. His gait was that of an Olympic sprinter as he rushed into the house to see Sarah bleeding from the shoulder, an unusual-looking knife lying on the floor.

His first thoughts were for Sarah, but as soon as he realized the wound was superficial and not as serious as the blood made it appear, he immediately sought the person responsible.

"Where is he? Where did he go? Are you all right?" David cried out, the veins in his neck extruding in the fight posture.

"I'll be fine," Sarah responded. "I'm more scared than anything. He heard your car coming into the driveway and ran out the back door. After that, I heard a car somewhere out in the field rev its motor and leave. He came at me just as I got out of the bed. As soon as I saw him, I immediately ran for the front door, screaming for you. At that point, he lunged for me and tripped over the ottoman in the living room. Thanks to that piece of furniture, I guess I'm still alive. Oh, David, I'm so afraid," she said, looking in the living room mirror at the site of where the knife had been lodged in her back.

"I'm so sorry I left this morning. I'm so sorry!" David said, thinking had he stayed with Sarah, this could never have happened.

"Oh, David, this is real, isn't it? Somebody does want me dead. What did I do to deserve this?" she cried.

David attended to her wound and immediately called Prefect Granger Bisset, who came to the property with Detective Alain Boucher.

"Do you feel up to answering some questions, Dr. Birch?" Granger asked while inspecting the shoulder wound. "Did you see the individual who did this?"

"Only from the back, Prefect. When David arrived, the intruder hightailed it out the back door. From that angle, he was a short, fat fellow who moved awfully fast despite the weight he carried."

"Where is the knife?" Detective Boucher inquired as he took measurements and sought any clues.

"It's still laying where it was dropped, Detective."

"That's an odd-looking knife," Detective Boucher remarked as he retrieved it.

"Let's have a look" Granger responded. "David, have you ever seen anything like this?" Granger asked, holding what appeared to be a sacrificial instrument.

"Yes, I have," David responded. "It was a long time ago back in my college days, when we visited the Guggenheim Museum in New York. If I recall correctly, that knife is a replica of the one used in the story of the binding of Isaac in Genesis, when God tells Abraham to sacrifice his only son."

"That's interesting," Granger replied, the significance of the knife rattling through his brain. "I suppose this antique knife may constitute symbolically just such a sacrifice, not of Abraham's son, a ram, if I recall my Bible correctly, but Sarah."

The interrogation lasted another thirty minutes, during which David showed his friend, the prefect, the notice that had been attached to his office door. He deliberately avoided allowing Sarah to read it.

Before leaving, Granger pulled David aside, leaving Sarah with Detective Boucher.

"I guess you now know this is pretty serious. I have always known we had some serious religious radicals around but not to this extent." Granger shook his head. "Over an overheard statement that was given to the news media, third or even fourth hand. Unbelievable in the twenty-first century."

David then told Granger about the Italian police providing protection while in Rome, as they had detected a death threat against Sarah.

"Also," he continued, "have you ever heard of the Holy Alliance?"

Granger thought for a moment and then said, "Yes, that was a group back some time ago that was formed for the protection of the crown heads of Europe. Why?"

"Well, according to Sarah's discussion with a priest named Gallucci Anselmo Brugundini, he contends this organization is still alive, doing secretive police work for the Vatican. He identified a Protestant group in Germany as the group that wants Sarah eliminated."

"Really?" Granger shook his head. "I never cease to be amazed at the power the Holy See can muster when it's necessary. I will have to look inti this Holy Alliance and see what light they can shed on this case. In the meantime, David, keep that little girl safe, and do not take any risks. I'm going to send out Officer Clermont to keep an eye on the two of you. Now I suggest you get Ms. Birch to the hospital and have that wound looked after. I will call them, so they don't think you're some type of madman who goes around sticking knives in their girlfriends."

"Thanks, Granger." David shook the prefect's hand. "I appreciate all you have done for us."

While Sarah's wound was being attended to by members of the hospital staff, David used the time to review the mail he had retrieved earlier that morning. Most of the postings were of the junk mail variety and were summarily discarded. However, one piece stood out with the officious-looking logo of the state of Sudan, a secretary eagle bearing the motto of Victory is Ours.'

It took only three seconds for David to open the envelope and realize the contents contained a job offer for the position discussed with the UNESCO representative. Despite the morning events, it was difficult for him not to be excited, as the offer contained everything any archeologist could want as the individual responsible for such a prestigious and esteemed position.

Now, he thought, *I have to somehow convince Sarah to see the advantages of agreeing to accompany me there as my wife.*

Little did he know the same issue had been on her mind since the enlightenment by Father Anselmo.

29

The evening on the town of Aix-en-Provence was interesting and fun, but Officer Clermont was never less than fifteen feet behind David and Sarah.

"What do you have on your mind that's bothering you so much tonight?" Sarah asked David when seated in the restaurant, recognizing his idiosyncratic mood swing, especially when Officer Clermont was listening to the conversation between them.

At that point, David uncharacteristically turned to Clermont and asked her to kindly leave the area so he and Sarah could discuss some personal items.

"Oui, Monsieur," she responded as she surveyed the dining room, looking for any signs of behavior that would be considered unordinary activities of either patrons or the service staff.

"I will be only a short distance away, and should you require any assistance, just yell out, and I will be here," she informed them in her most proficient manner.

"Thank God." David let out a sigh of relief. "I didn't think I was ever going to have any time alone with you."

"Why, David, she's only doing her job," Sarah responded, feeling a bit sorry for the officer.

"I apologize if I was a little terse with her, but I have something private to ask you, and I have some private information to share with you. First, let me say I have the opportunity to take the position in the Sudan that I told you about some time ago when we first met."

"I know," Sarah said. "I mean I know you were interested in the job, but you got it, that's great," she corrected herself, hoping to downplay her enthusiastic faux pas.

"Yes, it's a wonderful opportunity and one I'm sure any archeologist would find attractive, but there is a major obstacle." He pressed his lips together and grimaced, as if the problem might be insurmountable. "You see, I have this thing in my pants that is driving me crazy because I need to find a place tonight where I can put it."

"No wonder you wanted Officer Clermont to leave the area!" She laughed. "You are a dirty old man."

"No, no, I mean this thing." He reached in his pocket and pulled out a blue velvet ring case displaying a brilliant two-karat diamond. "Will you marry me, Sarah?" He watched her composure as he left his chair and knelt in front of her.

"Tell him yes," several patrons cried out.

"Tell him yes!" The chant began reverberating as David flushed in anticipation of Sarah's answer.

"I told you once before the answer to that question, and nothing has changed," Sarah replied, now becoming uneasy by the chanting of the restaurant patrons.

"Does that response also include following me to Africa and living in the Sudan?"

"Of course it does," Sarah replied under her breath while the chant was still going on. She then stood up while David remained in his kneeling position, and she, for the crowd's benefit, cried out, "Yes, yes, yes!"

30

Fourteen years had passed since David and Sarah committed themselves to a happy and productive alliance. Living in Meroe, just north of Khartoum, they had produced three children. Vickie was the oldest and was named after the woman who lost her life in what Sarah believed was a terrible misunderstanding on the part of whomever the shooter represented. Vickie was now ten years of age and was showing signs of wanting to follow in her mother's medical footprints. The other children, David and Jennifer, favored David and still had not exhibited any interest in either of their parents' occupations. David occasionally took them on field trips to "David's digs," as he called his work, and to Sarah's medical tours with Doctors without Borders. Oftentimes, these sojourns landed them in the depths of Sudan or in the surrounding countries of Egypt, Libya, Chad, Central African Republic, South Sudan, Ethiopia, and Eritrea.

As for Sarah and David, occasionally they would escape, taking advantage of daily flights to other far-flung destinations of Kenya, Tanzania and Zanzibar, Uganda, Ethiopia, or occasionally Dubai when, according to David, they were flush.

Sudan was not the most pleasurable of places due to the consistently high year-round heat, which made being outdoors often unbearable, even for the most athletic runners. Because of the heat and the children's well-being, David had a small thirty-six-thousand-gallon pool installed behind the living quarters. In time, it became the draw of the neighborhood, and the kids had more friends than they sometimes knew.

Also, because of the heat, David had installed two extra air-conditioning units, running constantly to cool the thirty-six-hundred-foot ranch-looking veranda circling the house he and Sarah had designed.

All in all, life was good for the couple, and the fears and concerns about the shooter had dissipated over the years, just as Father Anselmo had said they would.

"Have you been reading the news about this girl in Southern France who is doing some fantastic things?" David asked Sarah at breakfast.

"No, I can't say I have," she replied as the Muslim maid named Sahara poured her morning juice. After taking her first sip she asked, "Why? What has she done?"

"Apparently," David responded, looking over the top of the newspaper, "she has performed what some have considered to be miracles."

"Really? Whose definition of miracles? Some peasants or those of the church?" she said, the consummate research analyst, skeptical of any new enlightenment that was religiously oriented.

"I don't know. Why are you being such a snot?" David asked.

"I guess after all we have been through with the church, the DANNAR corporation, and the news agencies, I don't believe much of the bull and yellow journalism they invest themselves in. If it sells newspapers or puts people in the pews, they don't care whether whatever they're doing is right or not."

"Can't say I disagree with you there, hun, but this is a little different."

"How so?" Sarah now became inquisitive.

"First, the article identified the girl as an orphan but later indicated she and her parents, her mother and father, visited Rome, where they proceeded to lose her in the crowds near St. Peter's Basilica. When the police finally found her, three days later, she was sitting in the naïve of St. Peter's, surrounded by cardinals who were amazed at her knowledge of scriptures and of Christ's ministry on earth."

Twelve years ago, Sarah thought. Her birth date would just about coincide with the time she and Father Anselmo talked about the possibility that the church and the DANNAR corporation could produce a live and true replication of Jesus Christ. *Damn!* Sarah thought. *Could they have done it? Could this girl be the replicated one? A female Jesus. Wouldn't that set the church on its ear?* "So, what's her name? And where does she come from?" Sarah innocently asked as she came out of her temporary daze.

"It doesn't give too many particulars about who she is or where she comes from other than her name is Isa, and apparently she's a farm girl from the hills of Southern France whose education, at best skimpy, parallels Christ himself. The article only talks about some of the things she has done, most of which seem to parallel the early life of Christ as an individual. That's at least how the paper phrased it."

"In what respect?" Sara asked.

"Well, it seems she has been conducting some of Christ's miracles in the countryside of Southern France—Provence, if you believe that! People there say they are miracles that Jesus accomplished in his ministry." David read quips from the news article.

"Like what?" Sarah was engrossed further as her royal bloodline began to develop goose bumps over the thought this could be the real embodiment of Christ, the second coming brought on by the replication process.

"Apparently, this young woman has performed several acts that bear some likeness to those Christ performed in Galilee. For example, it says here that in one instance, a man with leprosy, who had emigrated to northern Spain from North Africa, came to her and begged her, on his knees, to cure him. Just as Christ did, the young lady became indignant with the man, not liking the fact that he attempted to goad her into healing him. Then, she apparently did heal him, telling the man to leave and tell no one. The leper agreed but instead spread the news that Isa had healed him. After that, she could no longer go to northern Spain for fear of being mauled for her special gifts." David put the paper down.

"In another, a man in her church addressed her as Isa, asking her if she had come to destroy them. The article goes on to say that Isa sternly said, 'Come out of him.' At that point, the impure spirit shook the man violently and came out of the man with a sound other parishioners dismissed as being unholy."

"So, what is the relationship with Christ?" Sarah asked?

"It seems that Christ had a similar incident that the article says can be found in the New Testament at Mark 1:23–28."

"Sounds to me as though the news media is jumping to conclusions. What do you think?" Sarah asked David, who was now looking up the biblical citation.

"There is some similarity between the newspaper article and what the Bible says," David advised Sarah after replacing the text back into the bookcase.

"So, do you think this may have some validity as to Anselmo and DANNAR?"

"I don't have any idea!" David shook his head as he moved to pour a Johnny Walker Black for himself and Sarah, replacing the traditional breakfast juice. "And even if it did, it's too little to make a snap decision on."

"Yes, I guess you're right. It wouldn't be pragmatic at this point, would it?" Sarah agreed, using her professorial vocabulary.

"I'll tell you what though. In the morning, as soon as I get to the dig, I'll use our international phone to call Father Jacques in Aix-en-Provence and get his take on Ms. Isa. If anyone knows about this woman, or should I say girl, the good Father Jacques Cronin will."

31

Early the following morning, as the couple was served their morning breakfast by their maid, Sahar, Sarah reminded David of the phone call to Father Jacques in Aix-en-Provence.

"Don't worry. I won't forget such an important and hopefully enlightening conversation with my old friend. Of course, I will have to wait a few hours until the time catches up. He's a couple time zones behind us," David offered as he grabbed his water bottle and floppy-brimmed hat. He made his way to the Land Rover parked in the driveway.

"OK, David," Sarah responded with an obvious look of anticipation. "I'm going into Khartoum today to do some work in the ER. Give me a call if you hear anything enlightening about this Isa girl."

"You're on," he said before the Land Rover carrying David made its way to the Meroe digs.

Three hours later, the phone in the rectory of Eglise Sant Joan rang, and it was answered by a woman who sounded as if she were a dowager empress.

"And may I say who is calling?" the woman asked.

"Of course," David replied. "Tell him it's his old buddy Dr. Behlke from Sudan."

"David, how are you? This must be serendipity. I was just talking about you the other day."

"By the way, who was that answering your phone? She sounded very old."

"She is old," the good priest replied. "You should remember her. That was Mrs. Pauget, our housekeeper."

"No kidding. She's still alive?" David said. "Guess I better be careful of what I say; it might wind up in the newspaper."

"Not necessarily," Father Jacques replied. "Her hearing is worse than mine nowadays, and she probably would miss 90 percent of what was being said."

"So, what brought you to be talking about me? Hope it was good," David said.

"Always, David, always. It had something to do with that problem we had here years back. You remember—about the second coming of Christ?" the priest asked.

"How could I forget what happened? That was the classic case of loose lips sink ships. I almost lost my fiancée because of your housekeeper's mouth."

"I know, I know," Father Jacques humbly replied. "That won't happen again. So, David, what is the reason for the call? It can't be social after so many years."

"Well, it really isn't. It has something to do with the very problem of fourteen years ago and the girl named Isa who is allegedly performing miracles in Provence," David stated with obvious concern.

"David, I don't know a great deal, but if you observe what has gone on here in Aix-en-Provence, you can start to piece things together and come to a reliable conclusion."

"Go on, Father. I'm all ears," David coached the priest, recognizing he was on a role and it was best just to sit back and listen.

"It all started after your abrupt departure and the move to Sudan. Shortly thereafter, there was a bonanza of archeologist priests representing the Holy See and a host of foreign digging companies showing up in Aix-en-Provence. They all had one common denominator, looking for the buried offspring of Mary Magdalene. According to old records and lore, her name was Sarah, the Jewish spelling meaning *princess*. For almost two years, the area was massaged by those looking for the lost princess. Then, one day, as fast as it had started, they all pulled out.

"Some said at that time they had found what they were seeking. That was basically it, but then about a year later, a child was seen at the shrine of Mary Magdalene. Over the years, the child, it was said, often indulged in some strange anomalies that resembled works of Jesus. After a time, the child vanished from the Magdalene shrine but resurfaced as an adopted child of a couple who made their home in the Provence Alps, in the spurs of the Maritime Alps, to the west of Aix."

Father Jacques paused, then continued. "I presume you must have seen the news article where the College of Cardinals fell over her as she preached the Catholic beliefs at St. Peter's Basilica in Rome."

"Yes, I did," David said, engrossed in Father Cronin's story.

"That, my boy, is just a small dose of the feats she has performed that someone could legitimately say follow Christ's story. Oh, and by the way, are you familiar with the name Isa, which she carries?"

"No, I can't say I am. It sounds Arabic, but I can't really interpret its meaning."

"You are right, David. It is Arabic, but it's old Arabic, and it's the feminine for Jesus."

"Oh my God," said David. "Is it possible the DANNAR corporation fulfilled the prophecy of the second coming?"

"I can't answer that question directly. I can only say that of the thirty-five miracles identified in Mathew, Mark, Luke, and John, she has accomplished twenty-eight, with, I'm sure, still more to come."

32

It was a mild spring Sunday morning when Isa arrived at the Fiumicino International Airport in Rome. It was her desire to attend Mass at the fountainhead of Christianity. She instructed a cab driver to take her to St. Peter's. Upon arrival, she was dropped off at Peter's Square, the large plaza located directly in front of St. Peter's Basilica in Vatican City.

As she began walking the roughly one-hundred-yard trek to the entrance of the church nave, she observed numerous vendors waiting to sell items to the Mass attendees.

Thus began an episode in the life of Isa that was out of character for her. Always so mild, composed, and considerate, upon viewing the vendors surrounding the plaza, she began accosting them and overturning the rosary seller's cart, confronting the vendors selling their hot, roasted chestnuts, those purporting to sell holy cards and pictures allegedly signed and blessed by the pope, and entire array of individuals waiting for the Mass participants to exit the basilica so they might descend upon them like locusts for their own benefit. "This is a house of worship to my Father," she shouted to the vendors, "not a place to make money and sell your trinkets. Leave this place!" she commanded them, just as Mathew 21 depicted: "Jesus entered the temple courts and drove out all who were buying and selling there, 'My house will be called a house of prayer.'"

As she entered the vestibule, she regained her composure, being inside the house of God. Mass had already begun at one of the forty-five altars therein, so she quietly took a seat and observed the beauty of the interior. Of particular interest was the

Pieta by Michelangelo. Its sight and the magnificent depiction of Mary holding her brought a tear to her eye. She was also impressed with the high altar sheltered by high columns and a canopy where only her successor, the pope, could celebrate Mass.

About twenty-five minutes into the proceedings, the offertory portion of the Mass was about to begin. At that time, a collection box began to be passed among the attendees. As the person passing the receiving basket reached the middle of the congregation, a shout rang out that mystified the attendees.

"In domo Patris mei mansions! In domo Patris mei mansions!" With so many incidents of mass shootings and church refinement in recent years, many of the attendees dove to the floor, hopefully removing themselves from harm's way.

The priest officiating the Mass looked for the individual making the foreign commentary and called out, "Who is it that dares to destroy these holy proceedings, and what is meant by your shouts?"

In response, several more calls were made, this time in Arabic, *"Lays fi bayt 'abi,"* Greek *"Όχι στο σπίτι του πατέρα μου,"* and finally, so all could know, in Italian, *"Non nella casa di mio padre,"* and English, "Not in my Father's house."

Isa stood and proudly responded to the priest's question. "My name is Isa Christie, and I am the one prophesized. You are desecrating my Father's house by this mindless pursuit of money during the business of allegedly honoring my Father. Your mindless desire for an offertory of money is keeping my poor people from feeling they are wanted." Isa visually reacted by turning the basket such that the money inside fell to the floor of the basilica.

By this time, the Gendarmerie Corps of Vatican City arrived and stood at the ready to restrain Isa as a mad woman, deranged and misguided.

Because nothing like this had ever happened in St. Peter's. The pope was advised and curious enough to see for himself the individual who could speak in a minimum of four languages words of Jesus Christ.

"Do you want this woman arrested?" the captain of the Gendarmerie asked.

"Yes," replied the priest who had been officiating the Mass.

"No," the pope replied. "There is something about her that is intriguing, and I would wish to speak with her.

"Who are you my dear?" the pope questioned.

"My name is Isa Christie, or, translated from an ancient Arabic language, Jesus Christ."

"But that is impossible, my dear. Jesus was a man" the Holy Father countered.

"No, Holy Father," Isa responded. "Jesus was all things, and most of what he preached has been tainted and lost. I am here to set the record straight and particularly to reinstate what the male society took from women at the Council of Nicaea."

"And what would that be?"

Isa looked at the pope and smiled, as if she knew some of the things that were immediately rushing through his mind.

"Well, if you have several days, we may be able to cover some of them, but for the sake of brevity, there are some things that come to mind, like the handling of Mary Magdalene, whose knowledge of my teachings were denied by your first pope, Peter. Peter was always a jealous man and did not care for Mary. With her knowledge and understanding of my teachings, she should have been the first pope.

"As for women in general, the church has many sins to be held accountable for. Before Nicaea, there were female bishops and priests in the imminent church. Decisions were made in unison between the sexes, no one was considered dominant. These relationships lasted for the first three hundred years after my time on earth. That is until the Roman influence and Nicaea relegated the woman to a subservient individual in the church's eyes. So, Father, as you can see, you have many sins to confess and rectify. The incident today of allowing people to stand outside the church so they may sell their wares and probably pay a fee to do so, and the many ways the church has money as their motivator is an insult to my Father and your God."

The pope turned and dismissed the Vatican guard, held out his hand to the young Isa, and invited her to accompany him so they could speak more fully about her concerns.

"I would be more than happy to accompany you to discuss my Father's wishes for you, the church, and the human race," Isa Christie replied as she extended her hand, which the pope bowed and kissed.

The Mass continued as people returned to their seats, but the mood had changed, as if a curtain had been pulled back, leaving sunlight in a dark room.

33

Civilization advances funeral by funeral.
—Margaret Mead

Much time had passed since the day when Isa Christie entered St. Peter's Basilica and placed her concerns about her Father's house before the hierarchy of the largest Christian assemblage in the world. That was almost eighteen years ago, and nothing had been heard from Isa since. I often wonder what happened to her and, particularly, to the complaints she laid before the pope.

As I sat brooding on the veranda of our home in Sudan, I thought of Isa's wonderment when she first realized that in her veins flowed the eternal liquid of the world—that she held the immortal bloodline of Christ. She had come a long way to the marble halls of Christianity, only to be swallowed by their grandeur and majesty. Maybe that is the price one pays. Dreams are like smoke emanating from a stack; they are immediately prevalent and then dissolve and vanish.

I often sit here and think about the events that led to my growth, which were dissuaded by finding Mary Magdalene, which led to my wonderful husband, David, and our three children, and the loss of a true friend, Vickie, who I think of often. And most significantly, my meeting with Father Jacques Cronin taught me that whatever my belief happened to be, it was right. It didn't have to conform with church cannons or, as he defined it, centuries of bullying, and finally, Father Anselmo, surprise, surprise, to whom I owe my life.

It has been a long journey, the likes of which seem hard to explain as I reminisce over the long years leading to my awakening. But most of all, I think of Isa. Where did she go? Did she lose her way? What happened to the question she laid before the pope about women in the church?

I can only imagine Isa's wonder when she first stepped off the plane in Rome. She had come a long way, and her dream must have been so close that she could hardly fail to grasp it. Maybe what she did not realize was that two thousand years of emotional bullying placed that dream behind her. As I sit here in the warm Sudan evening, I think of the women who lost when Isa entered the basilica.

Well, tomorrow is another day, and if my calculations are correct, it is just about the time Isa should be establishing her ministry. Who knows? Maybe someday Isa may reveal her truths!